Silent Bud Deadly

The English Cottage Garden Mysteries

Book Two

H.Y. Hanna

ISBN-13: 978-0-6484198-4-6

CONTENTS

CHAPTER ONE

Poppy Lancaster rose from her stooped position and groaned as she pressed a hand to her aching back. She felt as if she would never be able to stand up straight again. Gingerly, she rotated her shoulders, trying to ease the stiffness, and winced as a dull pain throbbed down her spine. *Owww!*

Wearily, she gazed around her, at the reasons she had been reduced to this state: weeds, weeds, weeds everywhere. Pushing through the grass, poking out from between the paving stones, thrusting up amongst the bushes and smothering all the flowers... She had been waging war on them since early this morning, armed with a hand hoe and weeding knife, but she was beginning to feel like it was a losing battle.

Sighing, Poppy leaned forwards once more and

tugged at a stubborn green tuft wedged between two large rocks. The leaves tore away from the base of the clump as she pulled, leaving the root firmly embedded in the crack.

"Aarrghh!" growled Poppy in frustration.

She shifted her position to crouch closer and grimaced as her thigh muscles protested. Then the sound of rustling behind her made her turn swiftly around. She was alone here at the back of the garden and her recent brush with a maniacal murderer had made her much more wary than she used to be.

The bushes rustled again, then parted, and Poppy smiled as she saw who had come to join her. If anyone had told her a month ago that she would give up her life in London to move to the country and fall in love with a smug, demanding, ginger-haired male, she would have rolled her eyes and laughed them out of the room. Of course, that was before she'd learned that she had inherited a cottage garden nursery, before she'd discovered secret green fingers, and before she'd met Oren.

Okay... the cottage garden had been so badly neglected, it looked like Tarzan (and several of his apes) could have set up home here; her fingers were probably still more yellow than green; and Oren was a cat—a big, handsome ginger tom, to be precise. He strolled up now and butted his head against her shins, giving his trademark meow which—to Poppy's ears—always sounded uncannily like he was saying "*N-ow?*" He twined himself between her legs, eyeing the limp pile of weeds and the disturbed earth around them with interest.

"Hey Oren... fancy lending me a paw?" asked Poppy.

"*N-ow?*"

Poppy laughed. "No time like the present. What else have you got to do anyway—wash your face?"

The ginger tom gave her a disdainful look, then stalked away to sit by a bush and pointedly began washing his ears. Poppy grinned and watched him for a moment, then turned to scan the garden around her again. The place still needed a lot of work—there were not just weeds to remove, but also overgrown shrubs to be trimmed, leaning roses to be staked, shrivelled flowers to be deadheaded, and wayward vines to be tied... but it was a vast improvement on when she'd moved in a couple of weeks ago.

She flashed back suddenly to the first day she had arrived at Hollyhock Cottage and stepped through that rickety front gate. Even in its wild, tangled state, the place had radiated a certain magic—an enchanted garden filled with treasures, and hidden from the outside world by the high limestone wall around the perimeter—and she had instantly fallen for its unruly charm.

But now she felt a familiar niggle of doubt. Had she done the right thing after all? A month ago, she'd had very different dreams—dreams of a life free from the drudgery of a dead-end job and the stress of crippling credit card debts, dreams of travel and excitement, and dreams of finding her father and belonging to a "family" at last. Oh, she'd always had her mother, of course—at least until Holly Lancaster had passed away last year—but despite the close bond between them, it had never felt complete. Poppy had always longed for more—for cousins and aunts and uncles and grandparents—the things that other people took for granted.

And while her mother's free-spirited nature and relaxed attitude to parenting meant that she'd treated Poppy more like a best friend than a daughter, there was one thing Holly Lancaster would never talk about: her family. So when a letter from a lawyer had come out of the blue, with an inheritance from a grandmother she had never known, Poppy had jumped at the chance to connect with her long-lost family and maybe even find her roots at last.

I just never expected to find my "roots" so literally, thought Poppy with a wry smile, looking down at the pile of weeds next to her, with their hairy roots bristling.

And it was up to her now to carry on the Lancaster legacy. In fact—Poppy smiled to herself—she had already started. When she had received the small sum of cash left after her grandmother's estate had been settled, the first thing she had done was rush out and buy a load of seeds. Then she had rummaged in the greenhouse extension at the back of the cottage—obviously added on by her grandmother to propagate and grow young plants for sale—and unearthed some seed trays, into which she had eagerly sown all the seeds. The wait after that had been tortuous, but the day she had noticed the first green shoots poking out of the soil had been the most exciting one of her life! And since then, she had been checking the seedlings impatiently every day, wishing they would grow faster.

In fact, I might go and check on them again now, thought Poppy, getting excitedly to her feet and making her way back to the cottage. She entered through the back door, which led directly into the greenhouse extension, and hurried up to the seed trays lined up on the long workbench in the centre of the room. But as she drew near, she caught her breath in dismay.

The seedlings, which had been so green, upright, and healthy yesterday, had all wilted and collapsed, their leaves yellowed and withering. A few stems had even blackened and begun to rot.

"No, no, no, no..." whispered Poppy, leaning down to look at them. "What's wrong? What happened?"

She inspected the other tray and the other... they all showed the same thing: every seedling had died or was dying. Poppy was filled with confusion and disappointment. What had she done wrong? She had faithfully followed the instructions on the seed packet—well, bar a few small things—and it had looked like everything was going so well...

Did I not give them enough water? Poppy rushed to fill a nearby watering can and began flooding the seed trays, only to pause and jerk back a moment later as she remembered the disaster she'd had with the office plants back in London. Those plants had nearly died because she had overwatered them. Maybe she had done the same thing here? But she had been so careful this time, feeling the soil with her fingers and making sure it felt dry before she had moistened it again...

Maybe they need more sun? She glanced doubtfully up at the glass roof of the greenhouse extension. Sunlight was pouring in through the glass panes, straight onto the seed trays. No, it couldn't be that...

Perhaps if I just leave them alone, they'll recover on their own, she thought at last with desperate optimism.

She forced herself to step back and, with a last lingering look at the seed trays, she left the greenhouse and went outside once more. Slowly, she walked back to the spot where she had been weeding. The garden seemed to close in around her, even more wild and tangled than it had been before, and she felt a flash of panic as the enormity of what she had taken on struck her again.

What had she been thinking? She had no plans, no skills, no real experience of gardening. She had nothing other than a few plant books left by her grandmother and a lifelong love of flowers. Why did she ever think she would be able to run a garden nursery?

Her anxiety deepened as she thought of the credit card bills she still had to pay off. She might have a place to live rent-free now but she still had to keep up the minimum payments on the credit card each month, and with no job and no income, how was she going to find the money? That bit of cash from the estate was only enough to tide her over for a few weeks, but after that?

A bee flew past her ear, buzzing merrily on its way back to its hive, and startling Poppy out of her agitated thoughts. She closed her eyes and took several deep, calming breaths. When she opened them again, she became aware of the faint sound of feline cries.

Oren! She looked around for the ginger tom. He was no longer by the bush, washing his face. Instead, cries were coming from the very back of the garden. Hurriedly, she pushed her way through the undergrowth, following the cries until she came to the walled corner at the rear of the garden. Growing against the limestone wall was a monster of a rosebush—no, not a bush, but a huge rambler with enormous thorny canes snaking out in all directions, like the tentacles of some spiny sea monster. Clusters of creamy-white flowers decorated the prickly stems that arched out across the tangled mass, so that it looked like the sea monster was covered in foam, having a bubble bath...

Poppy stared at it, wondering what to do. The rambler rose formed a huge mound, taller than her and several feet wide. Oren's cries were coming from deep in the spiky mass. Had he wriggled in somehow and then got stuck amongst the barbed branches?

"Oren? Are you there?"

"N-ow! N-oooow!"

"Hang on... I'm coming!" called Poppy

She reached forwards tentatively and tried to lift one of the stems. "Ouch!" She jerked back as a sharp thorn embedded itself in her thumb.

Poppy took a step back, sucking the wound on her thumb, and considered the monster plant again. She noticed a gap where its canes were draped over the wall on one side. The opening led into a hollow within the thicket of prickly branches. Slowly, she picked her way around until she reached the wall and, to her surprise, saw a wooden door through the opening.

For a moment, all the childhood stories she had read of fairy groves and secret hollows in enchanted forests ran through her head... then, as she looked closer, she realised that there was a much more prosaic explanation. The door belonged to an old wooden shed. The rose must have once been planted next to the shed and expected to grow up and cover the wooden roof in a pretty manner, but with time and neglect, it had just kept growing and growing, until it was now eating everything in that corner of the garden. In fact, if she hadn't come round to the side, next to the wall, she would never have even realised that there was a shed underneath.

Oren was standing outside the door, pawing at the wood and demanding for it to be opened.

"What do you want to go in there for?" Poppy asked. "It's just a dirty old shed, probably full of cobwebs and spiders…" She shuddered.

"*N-ow!*" said Oren, pawing eagerly again at the door. His tail twitched from side to side, and his whiskers quivered with excitement.

What on earth could be in an old shed that could get him so excited? Poppy wondered. Carefully ducking under a thorny stem, she went up to the door and tried the handle. To her surprise, the door wasn't locked, although it was stiff, the catch rusty. It took her several shoves to push it open. It swung inwards with a creak of the hinges that would have made any horror movie proud and Poppy felt an uneasy tingle creep up her spine, despite the sunny day.

She peered through the doorway but the brightness of the sunshine outside and the tangle of rose stems covering all the windows made it hard to see anything in the darkened interior. Poppy took a deep breath and stepped in. Slowly, her eyes acclimatised. The place was crammed with old pots and seed trays, metal tins and glass jars, coils of rubber hose and lengths of twine, rusty shovels, bags of what looked (and smelled) like dried manure, and an assortment of decaying leaves, twigs, and other junk.

Poppy took a few steps into the shed, wrinkling her nose at the musty smell. It looked like nobody had been in here for months: the cobwebs she had been dreading festooned every corner and a thick layer of dust lay on the potting bench by the window. Well, it was hardly surprising. With that thorny monster covering it on the outside, nobody would want to approach close enough to see the shed, never mind come in. Her heart sank at the thought of having to clear and sort out all this clutter and her first instinct was to back out and shut the door on all this mess. But before she could move, Oren streaked past her legs, making a beeline for the pile of burlap sacks in the corner.

He sniffed the pile intently, then looked at her over his shoulder. "*N-ow?*"

"No, Oren—we'll come back and sort things out another day," said Poppy, wanting to leave the grim, dusty interior and get back out into the bright sunshine.

The cat ignored her, pawing at the sacks instead. "*N-ow! N-ow!*"

Poppy frowned, then picked her away across the floor to the pile. "What is it?"

Oren jumped up onto the top of the pile and pawed at the sacks again, his claws hooking in the rough fabric. Poppy lifted a corner of the burlap but saw nothing.

"*N-owww!*" said Oren, climbing around the pile, his tail lashing with excitement.

Poppy exhaled in exasperation. "What, Oren? There's nothing here, just a heap of old sacks—"

She broke off suddenly as her ears caught a sound. She froze. Was that… *a squeak?*

Something moved in the pile. Poppy jerked her hand back, inadvertently knocking one of the burlap sacks off the top and exposing what was underneath. There was a scurry of movement, more squeaking, and Poppy found herself suddenly staring at several beady black eyes.

It was a nest of rats.

CHAPTER TWO

Poppy screamed involuntarily, stumbling backwards. "*Uuughh! Rats!*"

"*Yee-ooowww!*" cried Oren joyfully, pouncing straight on the nest.

Rats squealed in panic and poured, like lemmings, out of the nest and over the pile onto the floor. Poppy shrieked and hopped from foot to foot, amid the sea of furry brown bodies scurrying around her. Oren yowled in delight, chasing a rat in circles, then darted between her legs, tripping her badly. Poppy gasped, stumbled, and reeled backwards, crashing against the potting bench. There was an ominous cracking sound, and the next moment, the bench broke, sagging to one side and depositing her with a *thump* on the floor, followed by half the contents of the shed wall.

"Ow! Ugh! *Uummghph*!" mumbled Poppy as she was buried beneath an avalanche of empty pots, watering cans, rope, tools, twigs, and dried leaves.

Dust filled the air in great clouds. Poppy lay stunned for a moment, then gingerly moved her arms and legs. Nothing seemed broken. She sat up and patted her head, feeling for injuries. She exhaled in relief. Somehow, she had escaped unscathed—other than a few minor scratches, and several leaves and twigs in her hair. She turned to glare at Oren, who was standing a few feet away, watching her with what looked like a grin on his cheeky feline face.

"*N-ow?*"

"*N-OW* yourself," muttered Poppy, sticking her tongue out at the cat.

"What on earth are you doing?"

Poppy froze with her tongue still poking out of her mouth, then she twisted around as a shadow fell across the open shed door. The interior of the shed seemed to shrink as a tall man stepped inside. Dark eyes, saturnine features, a brooding, sensitive mouth...

Nick Forrest looked the epitome of the moody author—and he usually behaved like one too, swinging from friendly neighbour to scowling stranger in a matter of seconds. Today, though, he looked to be in an unusually good mood; he also looked like he was on the verge of laughter as he surveyed her dishevelled state.

"What does it look like I'm doing?" responded Poppy tartly, annoyed at being the subject of his amusement. Then she froze as she heard a rustle above her. Before she could react, a plastic bag fell with a *thump* on her head and split open, pouring compost all over her face and body.

"Ugh!" Poppy cried, coughing.

She glanced up, half expecting Nick to rush over with solicitous questions, but instead, the crime writer threw his head back and burst out laughing. He had a rich baritone laugh, with the same mesmerising quality as his voice—although right then, Poppy felt more peeved than enchanted.

"It's... it's not funny!" she spluttered.

"No, you're right... I'm sorry. That was ungallant of me," Nick said, although his voice was still unsteady as he hurriedly composed his face. He bent over her. "Are you all right? Can I help you up?"

Poppy scowled and ignored the hand he offered her, instead struggling to her feet by herself. She knew that she was being a bit silly—if she was honest, she had to admit that she would probably have laughed too if she had seen herself with a bag of compost on her head. It was just that... something about Nick Forrest always seemed to provoke her...

She dusted herself off and shook the compost out of her hair, then marched outside into the sunshine with Nick following. As they climbed out of the tangle of thorny rose stems and stepped into the light, she saw that he was looking suave and cool, in faded denim jeans and a V-neck cotton T-shirt that revealed his deep tan. The sight only made her more conscious of her dishevelled state and she felt her irritation increase.

"What are you doing here?" she demanded.

He raised his eyebrows slightly at her snappy tone and said, "I was out in the garden and heard someone screeching like a banshee next door, so I thought I'd better come and investigate."

"I was not screeching!" said Poppy. "I was just... uh... a bit startled." She gave him a challenging look. "I'll bet if *you* walked straight into a nest of rats, you wouldn't be so cool and blasé."

He grinned. "Well, actually, I like rodents. And rats are very maligned—they're incredibly intelligent, you know, and even..." he shot her a wicked look, "...quite cuddly."

Poppy was about to retort when she heard footsteps approaching. She turned to look at the path which led around the side of the cottage and out to the garden at the front. A man and woman appeared around the side of the house, coming down the path. He was in his late thirties, blond and good-looking in a superficial way, with pale-blue eyes behind trendy glasses and a stocky, muscular body tending to fat around the middle. She looked a good deal younger, fair and pretty, with the sort of peaches 'n' cream complexion that

Poppy had always envied. They were both dressed in smart casual clothing with the kind of luxury fabrics and tailored fit that screamed designer label, and even without the sight of the gold Rolex on the man's wrist and the pearls at the woman's throat, Poppy would have guessed that they were very wealthy.

"Nick, old man... you were gone so long, we wondered what had happened to you," drawled the man, coming up to join them.

His companion, who had lingered beside the path to look at various plants, joined them now, gushing: "Ohhh... this is just the most beautiful garden! Oh, darling, this is *exactly* the sort of thing I was showing you in *Country Garden Magazine*... remember? A traditional cottage garden, bursting with flowers, and all wild and romantic... oh, *look* at that rose climbing over the wall over there... and those gorgeous phlox under the honeysuckle... and the foxgloves... and delphiniums... oh, I just *love* it!"

"Don't stand there, sweetheart," the man said, frowning. "The sun is shining right on your face and you don't want to get freckles. Come over here—stand under this tree, where's there's shade. No, not there—that's *too* shady there... Here, come and stand beside me."

He reached out and put a hand under the woman's elbow, guiding her to his side. Poppy was slightly startled by his peremptory manner. He acted more like he was talking to a small child—or even a dog—than to a partner.

Nick cleared his throat. "Poppy—these are my friends, John and Amber Smitheringale. John and I used to be at Oxford together—he works in London now; he's a cardiologist and he's got rooms in Harley Street," he said, naming the exclusive area that housed the private clinics of England's most expensive medical specialists.

He turned to his friends and gestured towards Poppy. "This is my new neighbour, Poppy Lancaster. This is her grandmother's cottage, which she inherited a few weeks ago."

"Oooh! I saw the sign for *'HOLLYHOCK COTTAGE... Garden Nursery and Fresh Cut Flowers'* by the gate when we came in." Amber turned her big blue eyes on Poppy. "Your garden is simply marvellous!"

She beamed with simple, vacuous delight and Poppy felt a sense of unexpected pride. She looked around the garden again with new eyes. Having spent the past week yanking up weeds and fighting her way through tangled overgrowth, she had got used to looking at everything with a critical eye, seeing only the bad, the ugly, and the unwanted. But now she realised how much beauty there still was in the garden, despite the recent neglect.

Amber leaned forwards and said, "You have the kind of garden I've always dreamt of—I'm so jealous!"

"Th-thank you," said Poppy with surprised

pleasure. She'd never expected to be the envy of someone like Amber Smitheringale, who must have had everything money could buy and more. "Um... so what kind of garden do *you* have?"

The other girl dimpled. "Well, in London, we just have a courtyard behind our maisonette, but we've just bought a fabulous house on the other side of the village. On the outskirts. It's going to be our country retreat and it comes with a *proper* garden." Then she pulled a face. "Although... the previous owners must have wanted to live on a golf course or something, because the whole place was just covered in lawn! But I've had most of the grass ripped out at the back and new beds put in, and now I'm just about to start planting. I want to put in rosebushes and—"

"*You* are not planting anything, sweetheart," cut in John Smitheringale. "You're not laying a single finger on a spade." He put a hand on her abdomen. "We're not taking any risks with the baby and strenuous activity like gardening is out of the question."

Amber pouted prettily. "Oh, but darling—who's going to plant up the garden then? I wanted it finished before the end of the month. We're having the Fitzgeralds and the Somersby-Beales down for the weekend, remember? And then *Society Madam* magazine is doing a feature on us, and we *have* to have the house looking fabulous by then!"

"We'll find a labourer," said her husband, curling

his lip. “Some pleb who can come and do the dirty work.”

Nick cleared his throat, looking embarrassed by his friend’s rudeness. “There are a lot of landscaping services around these days. I’m sure they’d be happy to come and do your garden for you—”

“Oh no—I don’t want somebody coming and imposing their fancy ideas all over my garden!” cried Amber. “I know about landscapers. Christine kept recommending several companies that she’d worked with—”

“Christine?” asked Nick.

“She’s our interior designer,” said John quickly. “She’s been the person handling the whole renovation and overseeing all the décor and furniture choices for our new place.”

“Christine’s nice... but she has very modern taste,” said Amber with a peevish look. “I had to fight her all the way to get my ‘country kitchen’ and I’m sure any landscaper she uses would want feature walls with vertical gardens and concrete everywhere... They’d probably even want to install artificial grass!” She gave an exaggerated shudder. “I don’t care if it’s not trendy; I want an old-fashioned cottage garden—”

“I love that kind of garden too,” Poppy spoke up impulsively. “I’ve never liked the modern, minimalist look either, even though it’s supposed to be much lower maintenance. There’s just nothing like the romance of an English cottage garden with climbing roses and scented herbs—"

"*Yes!*" cried Amber, clasping Poppy's hands in both of hers. "You know *exactly* what I mean. I wish those landscapers could—Wait! I've just had the most brilliant idea!" She leaned forwards, her eyes sparkling. "Why don't *you* come and help me plant my garden?"

"M-me?" stammered Poppy, taken completely by surprise.

"Yes, I know what kind of look I want and where I want stuff to go—I've even bought some of the plants. I just need someone to do the actual digging and planting for me. You can help me do that, can't you?" She turned to her husband. "Can't she?"

"As long as Poppy does all the work and you just supervise," John said. "And she can also trim the hedges and rake up all the fallen leaves down the side of the house, while she's at it. I was going to get Joe to do that, but if she's going to be there anyway, she might as well."

Poppy felt a prickle of irritation. He was talking over her head and hadn't even checked with her first to see if she would accept the job! In any case, she couldn't take it—she had no experience of landscaping or any kind of gardening work. The most gardening she had ever done was just in the past week, weeding and tidying up at Hollyhock Cottage.

She cleared her throat. "Thanks for the offer, but

actually I don't—" but before she could say more, John cut her off.

"Don't fret. If it's an issue of money, we'll pay you very well," he drawled. "In fact, I'll pay you a generous deposit upfront, to get you started," he added, with the confidence of a man used to always getting what he wanted, provided enough money was offered.

Then he named a sum which made her eyes nearly pop out. Poppy swallowed and did some rapid mental calculations. With this money, she would have more than enough to pay the monthly minimum on the credit card bills for a while, plus have some left over to buy new seeds and other plant stock. Her protests died on her lips. She just couldn't afford to pass up this chance. *Anyway, it can't be that hard, can it?* she reasoned. It wasn't like she was having to plant seeds and raise seedlings—it sounded like Amber had already bought most of her plants in pots, ready to go into the ground. All she had to do was dig some holes and plop them in.

"Um... right! Yes, that sounds good," she said brightly. "When would you like me to start?"

"Tomorrow!" Amber beamed. "Can you come over first thing?"

"Sure. What's the address?"

As Amber gave her the details, a familiar feline shape appeared suddenly out of the bushes. Oren had been noticeably absent for the last few minutes—no doubt busy chasing rats all over the garden—but now he strolled over to join them, announcing his arrival with characteristic fanfare.

"*N-ow... N-ow...!*"

"Ugh! Is that your cat, Nick?" demanded John.

"Yes, that's Oren," Nick replied.

John grabbed his wife's arm and jerked her away, pushing her behind him as if protecting her from a sabre-toothed tiger.

Nick gave his friend an impatient look. "He doesn't bite."

"No, but cats carry toxoplasma—that can damage an unborn baby. I don't want him anywhere near Amber!"

Nick frowned. "As far as I understand, you can only get infected by toxoplasma if you handle cat faeces without washing your hands, or if you eat meat with the bacteria."

But John wasn't listening—he was too busy feigning a kick in the ginger tom's direction. "Get away... you filthy beast!"

"Hey, no need for that," said Nick sharply. He scooped Oren up and draped the cat across his shoulders.

Poppy was surprised by his protective manner. Her mercurial neighbour always seemed to treat Oren with a scornful impatience—and vice versa. In fact, the two of them were like a pair of grouchy old men living together, always winding each other up.

And yet now, as she watched Nick absent-mindedly scratch Oren's chin and the orange tomcat nuzzle his hand, purring loudly, she began to think that the constant bickering probably disguised a deep mutual affection. Not that either would admit to it!

CHAPTER THREE

Poppy had planned to spend the afternoon tackling more weeding, but with her aching back and sore muscles really beginning to protest, she decided to stop for the day. Besides, a part of her couldn't stop thinking about the dying seedlings. She had gone back in several times all morning to check on them but, by that afternoon, even a blind man could have seen that they were goners. She yanked the shrivelled little seedlings out of the trays and chucked them in the bin, then pondered what to do next.

I'll just try again, she thought cheerfully. *They were probably a bad batch of seeds or something. I'll just make sure I check the quality next time.* She thought suddenly of her new "gardening job" at the Smitheringales' and the extra money coming in, and felt a little thrill of excitement. Why didn't she go and buy some new seeds now?

An hour later found her happily browsing through the "Seeds" section of the nearest garden centre. She selected several packets and took them to the cash desk. There was a woman in a green smock behind the till, whose stern face didn't really encourage conversation, but Poppy gave her a winsome smile and asked:

"Is there any way of checking that the seeds in these packets are okay?"

The woman scowled at her. "Okay? What do you mean 'okay'?"

"Well, that they're... you know, good quality."

The woman bristled. "All our seeds are good quality."

"Yes, but... I got some from here the other day and the seedlings came up all right, but then after a week or so, they all died."

"That's nothing to do with the quality of our seeds. That's to do with your poor growing technique," said the woman with a disdainful sniff.

"I looked after them really well!" Poppy protested. "I followed the instructions on the packet and they sprouted and were growing nicely, healthy and green... and then, all of a sudden, they just wilted and went all yellow and rotten."

"Hmm... sounds like damping off to me."

"Damping off?"

"It's a disease that affects seedlings. They're

literally fine one day and dead the next. But it's nothing to do with the quality of the seeds—it's due to a fungus in the soil which attacks them—and *that's* usually caused by poor management." She gave Poppy a hard look. "Did you use sterile potting compost?"

Poppy looked at her blankly. "No, I didn't have any and I thought the soil from the garden would be just as fine—"

"*What?*" The woman spluttered. "No wonder your seedlings died! You *never* use garden soil in a pot—it's full of potential pathogens, plus it doesn't drain properly so it remains soggy, which just contributes even more to the growth of fungi. You need to use specially formulated, sterile potting mix. What about spacing—did you thin the seedlings out to prevent overcrowding?"

"N-no," said Poppy. "I didn't realise you had to."

"And watering?"

"Oh, I felt the soil with my finger every time before I watered," said Poppy, eager to show that she did know how to do *something* right.

"Yes, but *when* in the day did you water?"

"Oh… usually last thing at night before I went to bed."

"And I'll bet you used a watering can and poured water on them from overhead, didn't you?"

"Wasn't I suppose to?"

The woman gave another exaggerated sigh. "No, you never water from overhead if you can help it, and if you have to, you do it early in the day so that the leaves have time to dry off. Having wet leaves, especially overnight, is the perfect condition for all sorts of fungal diseases to develop."

Seeing the expression on Poppy's face, she relented slightly and said, "It's all right. We all make mistakes as beginners. You can try again with a fresh batch of seeds. You'll probably still get some seedlings that will die—that's just natural attrition—but you should get a decent number that grow on to be healthy plants."

"Okay," said Poppy, feeling more encouraged. She gave the woman a grateful smile. "Thanks for explaining all that to me."

She left the garden centre a few minutes later clutching her new batch of seeds and a small bag of potting mix, and walked to the nearby bus stop. As she waited impatiently for the next bus that would take her back to the village of Bunnington, where Hollyhock Cottage was situated, Poppy began to wonder if she should invest in an alternative means of transport. Now that she had decided to stay and make her life here, it made sense to have her own vehicle, so that she wouldn't always have to rely on the slow local buses. A car would be too expensive but maybe... a bicycle?

She looked up as a bus drew near the stop. The sign above the driver read "OXFORD" and, on an impulse, Poppy hopped on. She knew that the home of the famous university was a city of bicycles—it was what the students, university staff, and local residents used to get around—and she was sure that there would be good second-hand bikes at reasonable prices. She was free this afternoon; she might as well pop over and have a look.

The ride to Oxford seemed to take forever, as the bus seemed to stop in every town and village in the south Oxfordshire countryside, and Poppy was relieved when the iconic "dreaming spires" of the university city came into view. She alighted and asked around, and was directed towards the north-eastern end of the city, where the science departments sprawled around the University Park and where a popular bike shop frequented by students was supposedly situated down a side street.

It didn't prove as easy to find as the directions had suggested, however, and Poppy found herself wandering in circles, getting increasingly frustrated. At last, she stopped beside a sandwich shop and asked a freckle-faced student who was coming out, clutching a paper bag.

"Oh, you've got to go right to the end of this street," he said, turning and pointing. "It's the last shop on the right."

Poppy thanked him and was about to set off when she caught sight of the freshly filled baguettes displayed in the sandwich shop window. They all looked delicious and her eyes lingered over the mouth-watering labels:

Mmmm... "Roast Turkey with Crispy Bacon & Salad"... "Smoked Salmon with Fresh Dill & Cream Cheese"... "Honey-Glazed Ham with Tomato & Dijon Mustard"...

It was almost teatime now and the measly homemade sandwich she'd had at noon seemed very far away. Making a decision, Poppy turned to go into the shop—then paused as she caught sight of a man coming down the opposite side of the street. It was John Smitheringale. She started to raise a hand and call out a greeting, but stopped as she noticed that he seemed to be walking in a hurried, almost furtive manner. She wondered suddenly what he was doing in Oxford. The afternoon sun lit the other side of the street brightly, throwing this side into shadow—which was probably why he hadn't seen her—and Poppy instinctively moved back even farther so that her face was hidden by the low shop awning.

As she watched, John walked up to a door on the other side of the street—a classic Georgian door with a large brass knocker—which led into the multi-levelled townhouse almost exactly opposite the sandwich shop. It might have once been the home of a wealthy merchant, but it had obviously been converted and now housed separate offices throughout its different storeys.

There was an intercom mounted beside the door, above a gleaming bank of brass labels—the kind that was usually engraved with the name of the business or organisation. John threw another nervous look over his shoulder, then he hunched forwards, his whole demeanour that of a man trying to attract as little attention as possible, and jabbed his thumb on one of the intercom buttons. Poppy strained her ears as he leaned close to speak into the intercom, but he was keeping his voice low and he was too far away for the sound to carry. A moment later, the door buzzed open and he disappeared into the building.

She stared at the closed door on the other side of the street. *There is nothing odd about a man buzzing an intercom and going into a building*, Poppy told herself firmly. And besides, it was really none of her business. Still, for some reason, she felt an overwhelming surge of curiosity about what business or office John Smitheringale had gone to visit. Ignoring her growling stomach, she started to cross the street to get a closer look at those brass labels, but she had barely stepped off the curb when a bicycle came careering out of nowhere and nearly crashed into her.

Poppy gasped and jerked back just in time, while the bike came to a stop with a screech of the brakes and tilted precariously against the curb—or at least, Poppy guessed that it was a bicycle. It did have two wheels, although the front wheel was much larger than the rear wheel, like a Victorian penny-farthing. Attached to the rear wheel were two sail-like objects which looked like fish fins protruding on either side, and a long telescope was mounted on the handlebars in front, sticking out like a knight's jousting lance. But strangest of all were the wheels themselves. They seemed to be... Poppy blinked and rubbed her eyes, then looked again. Yes, they were *square.*

Perched on the seat between the wheels was an old man with a wild mop of grey hair and twinkling brown eyes behind strange goggle-like spectacles. He wore an old-fashioned, three-piece brown tweed suit with a red spotted bowtie, and carried an ancient leather case and umbrella in one hand. A little black terrier poked its head out from the laundry basket attached to the front of the handlebars and gave an excited bark as it saw her.

The whole scene was so bizarre that Poppy would have been sure she was dreaming, if it weren't for the fact that she recognised the old man. It was Dr Bertram Noble—known to his friends as Bertie—who was her neighbour on the other side of Hollyhock Cottage.

"Poppy! Fancy meeting you here, my dear!" Bertie hurriedly dismounted and lifted the terrier out of the basket. The little dog scampered over to Poppy and jumped up, waving his front paws in the air.

"Ruff! Ruff-ruff!"

Poppy laughed and bent down to pat the little dog. "Hello, Einstein. What are you doing in town?"

"Ah... Einstein and I have come to see an old friend of mine down in the University Science Area," said Bertie. "Professor Dimitri Xanthopoulos—do you know him? Marvellous man! And top-notch physicist too—he devised a new formula to calculate the rotational kinetic energy of a single axis system, you know."

He leaned forwards and said in a loud whisper, "Between you and me, I'm not sure I agree with his assumptions about the Moment of Inertia, but it's a good working hypothesis, nevertheless." He leaned back again and said in a normal voice: "I wanted to show him my new invention—behold! The Quadracycle!" Bertie waved a hand with a flourish and beamed.

"Er... wow," said Poppy, thinking that conversations with Bertie always felt a bit like you were talking with a friendly alien who spoke a language you didn't understand.

He glanced at the sandwich shop next to them. "Ah! Were you thinking of purchasing a sandwich? Their 'Roast Turkey with Crispy Bacon' baguette is particularly good. It used to be one of my favourite choices for lunch—"

"Oh, did you used to come here?" said Poppy in surprise.

Bertie's face sobered and a sad, wistful look came into his eyes. "Yes. My old laboratory was just around the corner."

Poppy stared at him, thinking of the magazine article she'd found recently. It featured an old unsolved murder case from a few decades ago: a research student had died in suspicious circumstances in the university laboratories late one night, and "Dr Bertram Noble" had been named as one of the suspects. *No, it was "Professor Noble" then. Bertie had been a professor at the university,* she recalled.

She looked at the old man next to her and wondered what had really happened. She'd wanted to ask him ever since she'd read the article but could never seem to find the right moment. Although she and Bertie had struck up an instant friendship from the first time they met, Poppy still didn't know much about her eccentric neighbour. It was obvious that he was a brilliant scientist and a creative inventor (although he wasn't always quite in touch with the "real world" and his inventions could just as easily maim you as help you!) and he'd mentioned that he'd only moved into his house a month or so before she'd arrived. But beyond that, she had no idea of Bertie's background, his family, or even how he supported himself.

She had tried to broach the subject once or twice, but somehow had always been diverted onto something else. And to be honest, she also hesitated because she'd got the sense that there was something in Bertie's past that he might be sensitive about. As someone who was fiercely private about her own background, she didn't like to pry into other people's affairs without their invitation.

Still, this seems like a good opportunity—after all, he's *the one who brought it up,* thought Poppy. She cleared her throat and said: "Um... Bertie... so you were a professor at the university?"

He looked up, startled out of his thoughts. "Yes. I was head of the Department of Experimental Science."

"And... um... you said that's near here?"

He looked sad again. "No, the department is no longer. They shut it down when they terminated my contract."

"Oh." Poppy didn't know what to say. She hesitated, then said gently, "Was it... was it because of that student who was mur—I mean, who died?"

Bertie gave a great sigh. "Yes. Poor Patrick. He was a wonderful young man and had such potential."

Poppy wanted to ask more but something in Bertie's expression made her stop. Instead, she said: "So were you living in Oxford until recently, when you moved to Bunnington?"

"Oh no, I have been overseas, my dear, for many years. I only returned to England a few months ago."

Before Poppy could ask more, the weirdest noise suddenly blared from Bertie's person. It sounded like a cross between a giant spring bouncing up and down, and a slightly drunk cow. It made the very air around them seem to vibrate as it pulsed with a strange rhythm.

"What on earth is that?" Poppy exclaimed.

"Ah, that's my phone ringing," Bertie said proudly as he patted his various pockets, searching for his device.

"Your... your phone?"

"Yes, I've selected a piece of didgeridoo music as my ringtone. Isn't it marvellous?"

"Er..." Poppy struggled between politeness and honesty. "It's... um... very unusual."

Bertie fished the phone out of his inner jacket pocket at last. "I wanted to make sure that my phone didn't sound like anyone else's, so I'd never be confused about whether to answer it. I did consider using a vuvuzela... but I thought this sounded more melodic."

Bloody hell, I'd hate to hear what a "vuvuzela" sounds like, thought Poppy, turning away politely as Bertie answered the call.

"Ah... I'm afraid I must dash, my dear," said Bertie a moment later. He scooped Einstein up and deposited the terrier back in the laundry basket, where Poppy could also see several pairs of mismatched socks. "Make sure you ask for extra bacon when you order your baguette. *Toodle-oo*!"

And with a wave, he was gone, wobbling precariously down the street on his square-wheeled bicycle.

CHAPTER FOUR

The Smitheringales' new country home was on the very outskirts of the village, in a winding lane that continued on into the open countryside. There were only two houses on the lane, both next to each other, and it was impossible to miss the one that belonged to the wealthy London couple. It looked like something out of a glamorous magazine—a beautifully converted and luxuriously renovated old farmhouse, set in extensive gardens, surrounded by a neat hedge on either side. The previous owners had created a row of topiary around the manicured lawn at the front of the house and the whole effect was so neat and elegant that in spite of her normal preference for the wild, informal look, Poppy hoped Amber wouldn't want to change anything at the front.

She started up the path to the front door, then frowned as she heard the sound of raised voices. Turning, she followed the path that led to the rear of the property. She was just coming out around the corner of the house and stepping into the back garden when she saw John Smitheringale. Unlike yesterday in Oxford, though, the cardiologist was making no effort to keep his voice down. He was standing by a gap in the hedge which separated them from the neighbour's property, shouting at a middle-aged woman on the other side.

"...won't stand for your bloody meddling, do you hear me? I'll report you to the local council, see if I don't!" he shouted, his face red and angry.

"I have done nothing wrong," the woman retorted, sniffing disdainfully. "I am well within my rights to clip the hedge."

"Yes, but you don't have the right to clip it on *my* side of the boundary!" snarled John. "Don't think I don't know what you're doing! You're leaning over and cutting holes in my hedge, so you can peek through and spy on us."

"What an absurd idea!" said the woman. She raised the shears that she was holding and said, "I am merely tidying the hedge and keeping the edges neat. If *you* maintained your hedges properly, I wouldn't need to exert myself on your behalf."

"I do maintain my hedge!" John roared. He gestured to the gap. "But *this* is not maintenance—this is you desecrating plants on my property, just so you can snoop more easily." He leaned close and shook a fist in the woman's face. "I'm warning you, Valerie—don't push me or you'll be sorry!"

The woman looked unconcerned. "Oh, I think not. I think *you* are the one who's likely to be sorry, Dr Smitheringale. After all, you have to think of your addiction, hmm?"

John stopped dead in his tracks. He stared at the woman, his face white with fury. Poppy saw his hands clench into fists and his body twitched, as if he was struggling with violent impulses. "You... you bloody witch—"

"Darling, do you think we can—oh!" Amber Smitheringale came out of the other side of the house, wearing a pretty floral summer dress and a white apron. She smiled as she saw her husband with their neighbour, completely oblivious to the tension in the air, and called, "I'm sorry—am I interrupting something?"

John took a deep breath through his nose and exhaled through his mouth, making a visible effort to regain his composure.

"Er... no, sweetheart, not at all. Valerie and I were just discussing the hedge... but we've finished now," he added pointedly.

Valerie sniffed again, then deliberately reached forwards with her shears and snipped off another leaf from the Smitheringales' side. John bristled, but managed to hold his tongue. Instead, he turned his back on the woman and stalked towards the house.

Poppy realised suddenly that he would pass right by where she was standing and would probably see her. Not wanting the awkwardness of him knowing that she had witnessed the whole ugly scene, she turned and quickly made her way back to the street. Walking up to the front door again, she straightened her clothing, put on her best "professional smile", and rang the doorbell.

Amber opened the door a minute later. "Ah, Poppy—come in! Come in!"

Poppy stepped inside the foyer and looked around. As would have been expected with the Smitheringales' wealth, it was a luxuriously furnished house, with handmade furniture upholstered in sumptuous fabrics, intricate wood panelling, and ornate fittings. Genuine antiques and expensive ceramics graced the many shelves and alcoves, and original oil paintings and water colours adorned the walls.

She followed her hostess into the spacious sitting room with French doors that looked out on to the terrace and the sweeping back garden. Elegant wicker furniture stood on the terrace, and beyond that was a small stretch of lawn which wound between wide flower beds. The beds were currently bare and she could see a collection of potted plants sitting beside one of the beds, obviously waiting to be planted. Beyond the beds ran a row of hawthorn shrubs, forming a hedge which encircled the property.

Poppy caught a glimpse of Valerie still standing by the gap in the hedge. The woman was making cutting motions with her shears, but it was obvious that she was really peering avidly through the gap, straining to look through the French doors and into the Smitheringales' living room. Poppy felt a prickle of empathy for John. Much as she disliked the arrogant doctor, she would be annoyed too if she had such a nosy neighbour!

"Oh, it's that dreadful Valerie Winkle woman," said Amber, following the direction of Poppy's gaze. "She's *always* peering over the hedge and trying to see what we're doing or listening in to our conversations. It drives John batty. Last week, he caught her in our garden, going through our compost bin—can you believe it? She said she was checking to see that we were 'layering it properly'." Amber shook her head in disbelief. "And John just came in and told me that she's been hacking at our hedge again! He's already had words with her about that several times."

"She sounds like a nightmare," Poppy said. "It must be really frustrating for John if she's always hovering around him when he's trying to clip the hedge."

"Oh, John doesn't clip the hedge!" said Amber, giggling. "He wouldn't know one end of the pruning shears from the other. He doesn't touch a thing in the garden. We have a handyman who comes to mow the lawns, trim the hedges, and do the weeding."

"Oh, yes, that's right... he mentioned that yesterday," said Poppy, remembering. She glanced at Amber. "Um... wouldn't your handyman have helped you plant the beds—?"

Amber made a face. "I suppose... but Joe's a bit off-putting to work with. He's really hard to talk to, and besides, I don't think he'd have the patience to faff around the flowerbeds with me, trying different placements and colours. In fact, I've heard him speak quite sharply to Valerie when she tries to interfere." She sighed. "Maybe that's what I need to do: stand up to Valerie more. She never leaves me alone: every time I go out into the garden, she pops up out of nowhere and starts telling me what to do. She always thinks I'm doing everything wrong." She shook her head and laughed. "John gets so annoyed sometimes, he says that if we'd known Valerie was next door, we wouldn't have bought the house! Of course, he doesn't really mean it—we love it here."

She gave another sigh, but a happy one this time, as she looked out of the windows and gazed into the distance. Poppy followed her example and admired the view of the rolling fields beyond the hedge at the end of the property.

"It really is beautiful, isn't it?" said Amber. "Because we're at the edge of the village, there's nothing near us except open countryside—well, aside from the old bottling factory. There, you can just see it through the trees..." She pointed. "It's actually situated at the end of our lane—if you keep going past our house, the lane curves around and ends at the factory." She made a face. "It's a bit of an eyesore, isn't it? It only shut down recently. I heard in the village that the site has just been sold—they're going to put a modern housing development there instead. I hope it's not going to be horribly disruptive while the building work is going on..."

She turned away from the windows. "Anyway, come and sit down. I've made some Florentine biscuits, and Christine and I were just about to have some tea. You must join us! Then afterwards, we can go out together and I'll show you what I want done."

Amber led the way to a three-piece suite by the fireplace on the other side of the room and Poppy was surprised to realise that there was a woman sitting on the sofa. She had been sitting so quietly, she had practically blended into the background. She looked to be in her early forties, slim, with dark hair in a sleek bob, and thin, arched brows in a patrician face. She sat incredibly still, like a statue, and her face had the same blank smoothness of a marble bust, so that it was difficult to read any expression.

"This is Christine—Christine Inglewood," said Amber, pouring out a fresh cup of tea and handing it to Poppy. "Christine's our interior designer and...

well, general project manager, really. She's been coming out to the house almost daily the last few months and helping us oversee every detail of the renovation. I think she's been living in the house more than I have," she added, laughing.

The woman gave Poppy a polite smile which didn't quite reach her eyes. "How do you do?" she said in a cool voice, holding out a hand.

"Christine, this is Poppy Lancaster. She's got the cottage next door to Nick—you know, Nick Forrest, John's old university friend who lives on the other side of the village," Amber chattered on. "We met her yesterday when we went over to Nick's place. Oh, Christine, you should see her garden. It's absolutely gorgeous! It's exactly the kind of traditional cottage garden I was telling you about. There are roses everywhere and lavender and foxgloves and delphiniums and... oh, so many flowers! It's the most beautiful garden I've ever seen!"

"It was actually my grandmother who created the garden," Poppy admitted. "But I *have* been putting in a lot of work, trying to restore it to its former condition—it got really neglected during my grandmother's illness."

"Really? How nice of you," said Christine in a bored voice. "I have to say, I can't understand the appeal of grubbing about in the dirt all the time. As I keep telling Amber, if she would just let this landscaping company I know come in and redo the back garden, they would install a beautiful, low-maintenance garden in no time. Then she could simply sit back and relax, and enjoy the rest of the summer—instead of having to worry about digging and planting and all that hassle."

"Oh, but it's not a hassle when you enjoy it!" protested Amber. "People who like gardening don't want a 'low-maintenance' garden—the maintenance is the fun part! We like getting our hands dirty." She made a petulant sound. "Not that I'll be getting *my* hands dirty for a while. John won't let me do any more gardening now, so I can't dig or plant anything."

"What?" Christine paused in the act of raising her teacup to her lips. "You're not gardening anymore?"

Amber shook her head. "Not until the baby is born. He says I'm not allowed any strenuous activity."

"But... but that's ridiculous!" cried Christine. "The doctors haven't told you not to garden, have they? John is just being silly. You can't let him dictate to you like that. You enjoy gardening and you should be allowed to do it. A bit of digging and planting is very good exercise."

Poppy looked at the interior designer with some surprise. That was an about-turn! Two minutes ago, she had been encouraging Amber not to bother with "digging and planting and all that hassle"! Still, she couldn't help agreeing with the woman's feminist sentiments and felt a growing respect for her.

"Well... I don't know... I *have* promised John," said Amber, fidgeting with the ribbons on her dress. Then she brightened. "Anyway, it doesn't matter—Poppy is here! We've hired her to help me put the plants in the new flower beds. She can do all the digging and stuff, and I'll just supervise."

Christine looked at Poppy and there was a flash of pity in her eyes, which annoyed Poppy slightly. Was the woman feeling sorry for her, being paid to be Amber's lackey? *Well, she doesn't know what I'm getting paid—she wouldn't feel so sorry for me then,* thought Poppy smugly. Besides, money aside, Poppy felt very lucky to have someone as nice as Amber to work for. The other girl had such a sweet, childlike manner, you didn't really mind doing her bidding. It felt a bit like indulging a bossy five-year-old child. *And it could be a lot worse—I could have been hired by someone like Valerie Winkle!*

CHAPTER FIVE

Twenty minutes later, after several cups of tea and a biscuit pile that had been reduced to crumbs, Christine Inglewood took her leave and Poppy followed Amber out of the house.

"I thought John was here?" said Poppy, looking around the back garden as they stepped out onto the terrace.

"I did tell him to come and join us for tea, but he said he wanted to pop into the village to get something," said Amber. She rolled her eyes. "Between you and me, I think he's just trying to avoid Christine. They don't always see eye to eye and she can be quite outspoken, you know... and John doesn't like that."

No, he wouldn't, thought Poppy. An independent, capable woman who isn't afraid to contradict him or speak her mind must be anathema for a male chauvinist like John Smitheringale!

"They used to be friendlier, you know," Amber continued thoughtfully. "In fact, it was John who hired Christine. I think one of his colleagues recommended her. But since Easter, things have got quite frosty between them. John never told me, but I think they probably had a few bad rows when he came up to Oxfordshire to check on the progress of the house. He was doing it fairly often—every week really—and he often came back in a foul mood. Christine can be quite rigid, you see, and she doesn't like it if you question her decisions. Neither does John, really," said Amber with a laugh.

"He's lucky, then, that his wife is so easy-going," commented Poppy.

"Oh, I just really hate rows, you know. Besides, I find that there are other ways to get people to do things, without having to get into an argument with them," said Amber with a little smile. "You know what they say: you catch more flies with honey than vinegar!"

They'd arrived at the bed with the collection of potted plants alongside. It was next to the gap in the hedge and Poppy glanced warily around for Valerie, but thankfully the nosy neighbour was nowhere in sight. Perhaps she had gone into her house to have some tea as well, or perhaps she had even gone out. Poppy hoped fervently that it was the latter. The last thing she needed was for Valerie

Winkle to watch her while she worked!

Amber gestured to several of the pots which held small rosebushes. "I went to a specialist rose nursery last week and got these—aren't they gorgeous? They're only little now, of course, but they'll grow into big shrubs. You know about David Austin roses?"

Poppy tried to look knowledgeable. "Oh... er... yes, of course," she lied. She had done some frantic last-minute reading of her grandmother's plant books last night, to try and prepare for today—but it had felt a bit like trying to cram things the night before an exam that you hadn't studied for. She had felt completely overwhelmed and hadn't taken much in—and had even fallen asleep slumped over one of the huge tomes. She had skimmed the chapters on roses and vaguely remembered a mention of "David Austin" but couldn't recall any of the details now.

Glancing at one of the rosebushes which was sporting big ruffled blooms in a soft apricot shade, Poppy hazarded a guess: "Um... they're bred by a chap called David Austin and they're... er... they're known for being very fragrant...?"

"Yes, they have the most wonderful perfume! And they've got lovely full, cupped flowers, with lots and lots of petals... see?" Amber lifted one of the nodding blooms to show her. "But they're not really old—I mean, they've been bred to look like the antique roses, but they're actually hybrids between the old roses and modern roses. I just love their romantic look, don't you?" she gushed, sweeping a hand over the bushes. "I got two in pink—different shades—one in a soft apricot, one in cream, one in a dark purply red—and this one is a sort of buttery yellow. I can't wait to see them all blooming!"

Poppy nodded, getting caught up in the other girl's excitement. "Yes, they're going to look amazing. So... where would you like me to plant them?"

They spent the next ten minutes placing the pots around the bed and trying different combinations, according to the roses' heights and colours. It would have been great fun—except that Poppy had to keep fielding questions about things she had no knowledge of and faking an experience in gardening that she just didn't have.

It was stupid—she should have just confessed the truth. Amber seemed like a nice girl and would probably have been very understanding. But Poppy couldn't bear the humiliation of admitting that she was a complete beginner who knew practically nothing. Besides, although she was supposedly hired just to provide the manual labour, the Smitheringales might change their minds if they found out how ignorant she was—and she couldn't afford to lose the money from this job.

"So do you think I need to do anything to the soil before you start planting?" Amber asked, looking doubtfully at the empty flower bed.

Poppy stared at the area. *Oh God—what did I*

read last night about soil? She racked her brains, trying to remember. "Oh, er... no, I don't think so."

"You think the soil looks good?"

"Um... yes... I'm sure it'll be fine."

"Oh, whew! Because the place where I bought the roses kept banging on and on about 'improving the soil' and trying to sell me a bunch of things to add, like compost and manure and stuff. You know, sometimes these places just try to sell you things, to make more money—I'm so glad you're here and know better," said Amber, beaming.

Poppy swallowed uneasily.

"Okay, well, I'll let you get on with it. Oh, I've taken the spades and garden forks and other tools out of the shed for you. They're over there..." Amber pointed to several tools lying next to the pots. "And there's also a new set of hand tools—they're in that bag there."

Poppy looked askance at the cream-coloured pouch covered in a pink and white floral pattern, which looked like it would have been more at home in a Laura Ashley photoshoot than a muddy flower bed. The flap for the pouch had fallen open and she could see a set of hand tools inside, with wooden handles that matched the vintage country look.

Amber caught her expression and laughed. "I know—they almost look too pretty to use, don't they? Christine gave them to me this morning; she said it's the sort of 'English country look' which would match my planned cottage garden, better than the bright plastic handles on the ones I'd bought from the DIY store." Amber chuckled. "She looked so horrified when I showed them to her last week—I think they offended her designer sensibilities! She's incredibly fussy about everything always matching the style and look of the place... I suppose it's the decorator in her. Anyway, it was sweet of her, wasn't it?"

"Yes," agreed Poppy, feeling her liking for Christine Inglewood increasing. The woman might be a bit of a cold fish—and a bit obsessive about coordinating appearances—but it was ultimately a thoughtful gift. Her heart was obviously in the right place.

"Now, I'm going to make up a jug with a cool drink and bring it out to you with a glass, so you can help yourself whenever you like. Would lemon cordial suit you? Or I've got soda water... or soft drinks too, if you prefer..."

"No, lemon cordial sounds great. But you don't have to bother, honestly. I'm here to work, not be your guest!" said Poppy with a laugh. "I can just grab some water myself when I—"

"No, no, it'll be no bother! It makes me feel better—like I'm contributing in some way to the creation of this garden too, even if it's only in keeping you hydrated!" Amber giggled, then retreated to the house.

Left alone, Poppy surveyed the flower bed once more, wondering which end to start from. She would do the roses at the back of the border first, she decided, and plant the taller shrubs that were going around them as well. Then she would take a break before tackling the smaller plants for the front of the border. But first, she would mark out the areas she was going to plant—maybe she could draw circles in the soil with a hand fork...

She bent towards the pile of tools but hesitated as her hand hovered over the pretty floral pouch. She felt bad soiling the pristine tools. Besides... she smiled as she remembered suddenly that she had brought her own tools with her. They were things she had found in the greenhouse at the back of Hollyhock Cottage and they must have belonged to her grandmother.

Poppy unslung her own large canvas bag from her shoulder and rummaged inside, pulling out an old hand fork and a trowel. Their handles might have been faded and worn, and the metal edges stained with rust, but there was something lovely about the thought of using the very same tools that her grandmother had once used to tend her plants.

Poppy had barely started digging the first hole, however, when a nasal voice broke the silence. Her heart sank as she recognised it.

"Planting roses, are you? You'll want to dig a much deeper hole than that...*much* deeper. At least eighteen inches down and the same across. And I hope you're not planning to just plonk the roses from their pots straight into the holes? Have you hydrated them properly first?"

Poppy looked up to see Valerie Winkle on the other side of the hedge, watching her critically.

"Um... you mean, watered them?" she asked.

"Yes! It's important to water them thoroughly in their pots first, so that they're well hydrated before you plant them, and also water them really well for the first few days after they've gone into their new spots—especially if it's hot." Valerie leaned through the gap and peered at the flower bed. "Have you improved the soil? Doesn't look like it. You need to give the whole bed a good digging over with a fork to aerate the soil—look, it's all compacted there!—and mix in lots of compost and other organic matter." Valerie raised her eyebrows and made a loud *tsk-tsk-tsk* noise. "I heard that you run a plant nursery—I would have thought you'd know something basic like that."

Poppy flushed and glanced quickly over her shoulder, relieved that Amber wasn't there to hear Valerie's comments.

"I... I thought the soil looked fine," she faltered.

"Rubbish! You haven't got a clue," said Valerie. "What about manure? Have you mixed that into the soil around the hole for the roses? You haven't? And what about mycorrhizal fungi?"

What on earth are mycorrhizal fungi? wondered Poppy wildly. She wished desperately that Valerie would go away. Not only was the woman making her feel utterly incompetent, she was worried that

Amber would come back any moment and hear Valerie exposing her as a fake.

Poppy bent her head and doggedly worked her spade, hoping that her lack of response would persuade Valerie to shut up and go away. But the other woman didn't seem to get the hint. Instead, she leaned even farther over the hedge to peer at what Poppy was doing.

"That's not how you dig a hole! You need to push cleanly into the soil and lever up..." she said. "And you should really be using a fork, you know. You need to loosen the soil at the base of the hole, so that it's easier for the rose roots to penetrate and grow down into the earth... No, no, not like that! Look, I'll show you—"

Valerie stepped through the gap in the hedge and came forwards. Poppy sprang up, shooting a worried look over her shoulder.

"It's all right, I can manage. I don't need—"

"You want to plunge the fork into the soil, like this..." said Valerie, continuing as if Poppy had never spoken. She shoved Poppy out of the way so that she could crouch down next to the hole and bend over it with a hand fork. She began to jab the fork into the soft earth at the bottom of the hole, moving it forcefully around. "Hold the handle like this—a firm grip—and make sure you separate any clumps—"

"Uh... ok, thanks... that's great... Look, I appreciate your help and thank you for the tips...

but I think I can manage on my own now..." Poppy babbled, throwing anxious looks over her shoulder. Amber was going to come back out with the lemon cordial any moment now and she didn't want Valerie here lecturing her on everything she was doing wrong!

"PLEASE! Can you just let *me* do it now?" she said, her voice rising.

Her sharp tone seemed to have finally got through to Valerie. The other woman stopped, rose to her feet, then shrugged and stepped back to allow Poppy to return to her place next to the hole. Pointedly, Poppy turned her back and began digging again—although she *did* try to follow Valerie's advice and mimic her movements. She worked in blessed silence for a few minutes, although she was aware of Valerie's disapproving gaze on her the entire time. When the hole was finally big enough, Poppy lifted one of the potted roses and tried to pull it out of the pot by grasping the central stem.

"No, no, no!" Valerie cried, sounding horrified. "You never yank plants out of pots like that! That's why I told you to water the pot first—then the soil is nice and moist and you just have to tip it upside down, put your hand over the base of the plant—and slide it out gently, with the root ball all intact."

Poppy took a deep breath. The woman was annoying... but she seemed to know what she was talking about. Besides, yanking didn't seem to be doing much good, other than snapping off several leaves and stems. She turned the potted rose upside down and tried to slide it out as Valerie had described, but since she hadn't watered the pot first to wet the soil, it still didn't come easily. Loose soil fell everywhere as she struggled with the upside-down pot.

She could hear Valerie making disparaging noises again and she looked up, about to say something defensive, but her words died on her lips as she realised that the other woman was not making sounds of contempt but rather sounds of distress.

"Valerie...?" Poppy looked at her in sudden concern.

Valerie staggered slightly, then she doubled over with a moan.

"Oh my goodness... are you all right?" cried Poppy, her irritation forgotten. She dropped the rose and rushed over to the other woman.

Valerie made a flailing motion with one hand, her other hand going to clutch her chest. She seemed to be having difficulty breathing and her face was going purple.

"Is it your heart?" asked Poppy desperately. "Do you have a heart condition? Do you have any medication I can get you?"

Valerie tried to speak but only another moan escaped her lips. She staggered towards her own house, collapsing against the hedge as she tried to get through the gap. Poppy hurried to grasp her elbow and support her.

"Wait—let me... I'll help you back and then maybe we should call an ambulance—"

"Eeuu...uughh..."

Valerie was gasping and wheezing now, as if she couldn't breathe, and Poppy was beginning to get really alarmed. She wondered if she should run back into the Smitheringales' house to call an ambulance, but she was reluctant to leave the other woman alone. She started to ask again about any medication, but Valerie suddenly tore out of her grip and lurched towards her own house. She only managed a few steps, however, before she crumpled and collapsed on the grass.

"Valerie!"

Poppy ran after her and crouched down next to the prone woman. She bent to roll her over, then froze. Something about the unnatural stillness of the body made a chill of fear slide down her spine. She licked her lips.

"Valerie?"

Nothing. No sound came from the collapsed woman. Not even the sound of breathing.

Don't be ridiculous—of course she's still breathing! Poppy admonished herself. *I just can't hear it, that's all, because she's lying facedown in the grass. Once I turn her over...*

It took her a few minutes of heaving and shoving to roll the body over. Poppy sat back on her heels, panting, then swallowed uncomfortably as she looked down at Valerie's mask-like face. Slowly, she went through the motions of leaning close to listen for breathing, watching the woman's chest, feeling for her pulse... it was as if she knew the truth but just didn't want to admit it.

Valerie Winkle was dead.

CHAPTER SIX

"There's been another murder."

"What?" Nell's voice sounded shrill with disbelief. Then she gave a sigh. "Oh... you're having a laugh, aren't you?"

"No, I'm serious! Remember I told you about that couple who hired me to help plant their new garden? Well, I went over to their place to start work the day before yesterday and I met their neighbour, Valerie Winkle. She's—she was—this awful woman who kept sticking her nose in everywhere, and being really bossy and rude... honestly, Nell, she was unbelievable! She even cut holes in their hedge so that she could spy on them!"

Poppy took a breath and rushed on before Nell could comment. "Anyway, she came to watch me while I was planting the roses and she was really patronising, like lecturing me about how to dig the hole and everything... and then she started making these funny noises and staggering around. I thought she was having a heart attack or something, 'cos she was clutching her chest, and I was just about to run and call the ambulance when she dropped dead!"

"Oh my lordy Lord... Are you sure it *wasn't* just a heart attack?"

"Yes, I spoke to Suzanne this morning... You remember Suzanne Whittaker—Inspector Whittaker, that is? She's a detective with the South Oxfordshire CID—"

"Yes, she's your neighbour's old girlfriend, isn't she? The chap who's the crime writer... Nick What's-His-Name?" said Nell.

Poppy grinned. How like Nell to remember Nick and Suzanne's special relationship status. When she had been living in London and subletting rooms from Nell, her old friend and landlady had spent most of her free time speculating about the love lives of various neighbours and residents on their street. That was when her nose wasn't buried in a romance novel. If there was a love affair, a cheating scandal, a divorce, or a tragic case of unrequited love anywhere within sniffing distance, Nell would be sure to know all the details. Now she said, with that familiar inquisitive tone to her voice:

"Are you sure they're no longer together? Because from what you told me, they sound awfully chummy to be exes."

"Maybe they're just being mature and philosophical about it; you know, they agreed that it didn't work out and they've decided to move on and just be friends. I mean, people can still be civil and nice to each other, even if they're no longer in love."

"Don't you believe it," said Nell darkly. "Break-ups are always nasty and bitter, and people never forget—especially the one who was dumped. Anyway, they sound more than just civil... I mean, wasn't Suzanne going over to feed Nick's cat for him when he went on a book tour? And you said she had the keys to his house and invited you over without even asking him."

"Oh no, she did ask him first. She had the keys because *she* was supposed to be the one feeding his cat, but then she got the idea of me staying there instead. It made sense—it gave me a place to stay while the cottage was still a crime scene, and Suzanne didn't have to worry about coming over every day to feed the cat."

"But what about the night you arrived at the cottage? You said you saw them kissing—"

"I never said—!" Poppy gasped in exasperation. "It was just a peck on the cheek when she was saying goodbye to him. It was dark and I couldn't see very well—anyway, it's really none of our business!" she added, feeling uncomfortable to be discussing Nick and Suzanne this way. "We're not talking about their love life—we're talking about

Suzanne investigating Valerie Winkle's death, which is much more interesting!"

"Mmm..." said Nell, not sounding like she agreed. Still, she dropped the subject and said: "So what makes the police think it's murder?"

"There was poison in Valerie's system," said Poppy. "That's what Suzanne told me."

"Poison? *Really?*" Nell sounded more interested now.

"Yes, Suzanne thinks somebody put it into Valerie's food or drink."

"*Did* you see her eat or drink anything?"

"No. Although... she did disappear for a while after I saw her initially by the hedge. I remember thinking that she must have gone into her house for morning tea or something. It was around ten o'clock, so it would have been around the right time."

"Hmm... how do they know that it was poison?" Nell asked. "Maybe it was due to something from her garden instead. People never wash their hands properly, you know, and they don't wear gloves when they should, and there are so many germs in the soil—oh my lordy Lord, Poppy, I read an article in the paper the other day about a man who ended up in hospital intensive care, just because he got a scratch while gardening. It said there are all sorts of bacteria and fungi in the soil and if they get into your blood, you can get septic shock! That's what happened to him, poor chap. He nearly lost his life."

"Yes, but wouldn't that sort of thing take some time to develop?" argued Poppy. "I was standing there with Valerie and she was perfectly fine one moment—and then suddenly, she collapsed the next! That couldn't have been due to a bacterial infection, surely? She would have looked ill already."

"I suppose so..." Nell still sounded doubtful. As someone who was obsessive about cleaning, she just couldn't believe that bacteria weren't the root of all evil. "Are the police searching her house and testing everything in her kitchen?"

"Yes, I think so. I haven't been back to work at the Smitheringales' since the day it happened—Amber was too upset, and anyway, the police roped off the whole area as a crime scene. But they've released the section of the garden on the Smitheringales' side now so I'm going back today to continue where I left off."

"Well, you be careful now," said Nell. "Make sure you wear gloves all the time and maybe you shouldn't eat or drink anything while you're there—"

"Nell!" Poppy gave an exasperated laugh. "Valerie wasn't poisoned by John and Amber!"

"How do you know?"

"Well, I—" Poppy broke off as the memory of John's furious face came back to her. She thought of the ugly argument she had witnessed when she'd first arrived at the couple's house. And then she thought of John's strange absence during the tea with Christine. Had he really gone into the village? Or had he gone next door to poison Valerie Winkle's drink, to get rid of his annoying neighbour once and for all?

Don't be ridiculous, she admonished herself. *Lots of people don't get on with their neighbours, but they don't try to murder them!*

"Poppy?"

"Hi... yes, I'm here. Sorry, my mind wandered for a moment..."

"Are you thinking that the Smitheringales *could* have something to do with it?"

"No, no, of course not," said Poppy quickly. "It's absurd to think that they might try to poison their neighbour! Besides, Amber was with me and Christine the whole time, so she couldn't have been next door adding anything to Valerie's tea. And John... John went into the village."

"Well, I hope the police make an arrest quickly. I don't like the thought of you being up there in the cottage, all by yourself, with a murderer running loose—"

"Nell..." Poppy said with a mixture of affection and exasperation. "Don't worry! I'll be fine. It's perfectly safe, and anyway, it's nothing to do with me. I didn't even know Valerie—well, until the day before yesterday, anyway... Yes, of course I lock the doors at night... No, I always check before I open the door—I've got that peephole put in now, remember? Yes, yes, all right, I will... You take care as well now... I'll speak to you soon... Goodbye."

Poppy hung up and sat back with a fond smile on her face. Although she complained good-naturedly about the fussing, deep down she appreciated having the maternal presence that Nell provided in her life. Ever since she had lost her mother a year ago, she had been alone, with no other family, and it was lovely to feel that somebody cared for and worried about her.

In fact, Nell probably provided more nurturing than her own mother had ever done. Holly Lancaster had been an eternal wild-child, a reckless dreamer who had never really grown up, and half the time Poppy had felt like *she* was the one who had to look after her mother and not the other way around. When her mother died, she had been surprised to find that—despite the grief—she hadn't felt as alone as she'd thought she would, and she realised that it was because of Nell. The talkative cleaning lady, with her warm, maternal presence, had ceased to be just a friend and landlady, and had become "family". In fact, since moving to Oxfordshire, Poppy missed their daily talks and companionable evenings together, and now she promised herself that she would make a trip back to London as soon as she was able, to spend a bit of quality time with Nell.

***

Poppy stood on the Smitheringales' front porch and rang the doorbell, trying to ignore the sense of *déjà vu* that assailed her. It was heightened when Amber opened the door and greeted her with a warm smile, just like two days ago—although Poppy noticed that the other girl looked rather wan and her eyes were shadowed. She followed Amber through the house to the spacious living room with the French doors overlooking the rear gardens, and did a double take when she saw that—just like the other day—there was a tea service and a plate of biscuits on the coffee table, and a woman sitting on the sofa.

This time, the visitor was not Christine Inglewood, however. It was a woman that Poppy vaguely recognised as one of the village residents: Mrs Peabody—a nosy, talkative sort who always seemed to be hovering around the village green or gossiping in the post office shop. She looked up with interest now as Poppy came into the room and said in a loud voice:

"Ah! Poppy, isn't it? Mary Lancaster's long-lost granddaughter—come back to continue the family business! I knew your grandmother, you know. Very hard woman. Didn't have many friends in the village. But she was a marvel with the plants, I must say. I once took a dahlia into the nursery to ask her advice. Had it for five years and it had never bloomed once—not once!—and Mary said leave it with her. Went back a couple of weeks later and it was covered in flowers as big as dinner plates! Can you believe it? I hope you've inherited your grandmother's green fingers."

"Er... hello, Mrs Peabody..." said Poppy, giving the woman a hesitant smile. "How are you?"

"Fine, fine, never better. Just come back from a holiday on the Norfolk coast, you know. The sea air is very bracing up there. Cleans out your lungs wonderfully. But I was terribly shocked when I returned yesterday to hear about Valerie Winkle! I *had* to come over straight away to see Amber and make sure she was coping all right." She clasped a dramatic hand to her ample bosom. "Poisoned! Can you believe it? It's like something straight out of *Midsomer Murders*! And I believe you were there when it happened, my dear?" She leaned forwards, her eyes gleaming as she eyed Poppy like a delicious piece of cake she couldn't wait to eat.

Poppy shifted uncomfortably. "Um... yes, I was. I mean, not when she was poisoned—but I was there when Valerie became ill and collapsed."

"And I heard that it was out in the garden?" Mrs Peabody looked out of the French windows. "In *this* garden, rather than her own?" She turned back to look at Poppy questioningly.

"Um... yeah... Valerie had come over to... er... watch me plant the roses and then... she started to stagger around and have trouble breathing..." Poppy trailed off.

"Oh, it sounds horrid!" cried Amber. "I'm sure Poppy doesn't want to have to go over it all again."

Poppy gave her a grateful smile. "It's all right. I've had to repeat it a few times now, for the police and—"

"Ah, the police!" Mrs Peabody gave a coy smile. "Yes, they've been busy questioning everyone in the village, especially those who might have seen Valerie the day before yesterday."

"Have they got any suspects?" asked Amber.

"They've only just started the investigation," said Poppy. "Surely it's going to take them a while to make a list of people who could be the murderer?"

"On the contrary..." Mrs Peabody gave a smug smile. "I know exactly who wanted Valerie Winkle dead."

CHAPTER SEVEN

There was silence in the living room after Mrs Peabody's startling announcement and the woman leaned back on the sofa with a wide smile on her face, obviously enjoying her moment in the spotlight.

"Oh my God, you know who the murderer is?" squealed Amber. "Who?"

"Well, it's obvious, isn't it? Prunella Shaw!"

"Who's Prunella Shaw?" asked Poppy.

Mrs Peabody turned to her. "She's a resident of the village, dear. She lives in that big cottage in the lane behind the church."

"Oh... the one with the garden full of delphiniums?" cried Amber. "I've walked past her house a few times and her garden is just breathtaking! I've been meaning to pop in and ask her for some tips."

"Yes, the delphiniums are the point," said Mrs Peabody, nodding. "Prunella thinks that she grows the best delphiniums in the county—and the judges seem to agree. She is always awarded first prize for her flowers at the Oxfordshire Delphinium Society show each year... Well, every year except for this year," she said with a meaningful look.

"What happened this year?" asked Amber.

"Ah... well, this year, Valerie kept telling Prunella to give the plants some extra fertiliser just before the show. She insisted that it would help them bloom better, you see, and produce bigger flowers—but Prunella didn't agree. The two of them had quite a row about it, actually, in church one Sunday. In fact, they were making so much noise that the vicar had to ask them to leave before the end of the service. Then..." Mrs Peabody lowered her voice dramatically. "Valerie Winkle took it upon herself to sneak into Prunella's garden and pour fertiliser on the delphiniums being prepared for the show!"

"But... surely you're not suggesting that Prunella murdered her because of *that*," Amber protested. "People disagree about gardening all the time. Just because you don't like their gardening method doesn't mean that you'd murder them."

"It does when their gardening method causes you to lose your prize delphiniums!" retorted Mrs Peabody. "All of Prunella's plants suffered fertiliser burn—Valerie probably used too strong a mixture and didn't water it in properly afterwards—and they were ruined for the show. They literally shrivelled up and went yellow and their leaves fell off. A few of them even died. It was awful to see. Prunella was absolutely *livid.* I was there, in the post office shop, when she stormed in, and I thought she was going to kill Valerie with her bare hands! We had to call Eric from the pub to help drag her off."

"But... murder? Just because she didn't win at the show?" Amber still looked sceptical.

"You don't know Prunella like I do," said Mrs Peabody. "Winning that show is everything to her. She has won every year for the last decade and she can't bear to hurt that record. It's a point of pride for her that she maintains her reputation as the top delphinium exhibitor in the region. In fact, I remember one year, there was a real scandal because another exhibitor snipped off a couple of florets from Prunella's spike by mistake. Or at least, she said it was a mistake—but Prunella was convinced the woman had done it on purpose and she flew into a total rage. She threw a watering can at the woman's head."

"Bloody hell!" said Poppy. "Was the woman all right?"

"Well, luckily Prunella's aim was pretty poor and all that happened was that the woman got drenched. Still, it tells you that Prunella can get violent when she loses her temper, doesn't it?" said Mrs Peabody with an arch look.

"Have you told the police this?" asked Poppy.

"Of course! I told Inspector Whittaker everything yesterday afternoon when the police were holding those interview sessions in the village pub. She was very grateful for the information," said Mrs Peabody, glowing with self-importance. "She said she would question Prunella right away. I wouldn't be surprised if she makes an arrest today."

"Oh, that would be wonderful!" cried Amber. "It would be a relief to know that they've found the murderer."

Poppy said nothing. Somehow, she didn't think things would be so simple and straightforward.

***

Poppy excused herself as soon as politeness allowed and headed out to the Smitheringales' back garden, glad that she had an excuse to escape Mrs Peabody's nosy questions. She walked over to the flower bed she had been working on and stood for a moment surveying it. She couldn't help thinking of Valerie and she glanced over at the murdered woman's house. The front door was still barred by the blue-and-white police tape, and there were obvious signs that the forensics team had been taking samples from the dead woman's garden.

Poppy felt a sudden flash of remorse as she thought of the dismissive way she had treated Valerie that morning. Yes, the woman had been incredibly annoying but still... *Could she have been saved if I'd noticed her distress earlier?* Poppy wondered guiltily. She felt terrible now that she hadn't paid more attention to Valerie; she couldn't shake off the feeling that perhaps she might have "done more" and prevented the terrible tragedy from happening.

Well, it's too late for regrets now—but there is still something I can *do*, she thought grimly. *I can help to find Valerie's killer and bring him to justice.* She thought back to the conversation with Mrs Peabody and wondered if the murderer really could be Prunella Shaw. She had seen first-hand how annoying Valerie had been with her know-it-all attitude and bossy manner—and in this case, it had cost Prunella her prized flowers—but still, it seemed like such a far-fetched motive.

But if it wasn't Prunella, then who? John Smitheringale? Poppy frowned as she thought of the arrogant cardiologist. Wouldn't his motive be even more far-fetched? People didn't commit murder just because their neighbour cut a hole in their hedge!

With a sigh, she turned back to the flower bed and reminded herself that her first job was to be a gardener, not a detective. She found the rose that she had been trying to plant that morning, still half-in and half-out of its pot. It looked a bit worse for wear now—a lot of soil had been knocked out of its pot when it had been turned upside down and Poppy could see several of the roots exposed. The stems were all limp, the leaves wilting, and the beautiful pink blooms were shrivelling up, the petals falling off and scattering everywhere. She felt guilty that she had just left it where she had dropped it and completely forgotten to check on it over the last two days. Hurriedly, she poured some water onto the rose, then went around and watered all the other pots as well.

Poppy spent the rest of the morning digging holes and planting roses. She did wonder if she should have spent time working the soil in the flower beds first, adding organic matter like manure and compost, as Valerie had suggested. But she was impatient to get the roses in the ground and she could always add the compost later, she reasoned. Besides, how did she know that Valerie really knew what she was talking about? Look what had happened to Prunella's delphiniums, all because Valerie had had completely the wrong idea!

Poppy worked happily all day and was so engrossed in what she was doing that she barely noticed the hours passing. Very soon, the sun began to slip down the horizon. She stood back and stretched her aching muscles as she surveyed the flower bed again, this time with great satisfaction. Everything looked great! Instead of a bare expanse of earth, there were now clumps of green strategically placed around the bed. There were still big gaps to fill, and she hadn't finished planting all the pots, but already it was beginning to look more like a "real" garden.

Feeling flushed with pride, Poppy gathered her things, tidied up the empty pots, and returned the spade to the pile of tools by the hedge. Then she bade Amber goodbye and headed back to the other side of the village. As she walked down the cul-de-sac to Hollyhock Cottage and passed Nick's house, which was the property just before hers, a svelte shape detached itself from the shadows next to the gate and strolled across her path.

"*N-ow…?*" said Oren, flicking his striped orange tail.

"Hello, you…" said Poppy, breaking into a smile as she paused to pat the cat. "What are you doing out here?"

Oren purred loudly, rubbing his chin against her knee. From her recent experience pet-sitting him, she knew that the ginger tom was probably asking for food. He had a ravenous appetite and usually started hassling people for his dinner from early in the afternoon. She glanced up at the darkened house next to them, wondering where Nick was.

"I'm sure he'll be back soon and he'll feed you then," she said.

"N-ow! N-ow!" insisted Oren.

Poppy looked at the empty house again, then said: "Oh, all right. But don't tell Nick!" and—against her better judgement—she scooped the cat up and carried him back to Hollyhock Cottage.

Depositing him in the kitchen, she rummaged in the pantry and pulled out a tin of cat food. It had been an impulse buy the last time she was in the supermarket, and as she tackled it with a tin opener, she felt slightly guilty. She shouldn't really have been feeding Oren—she knew that he was amply fed at home. Still, she just couldn't bear the thought of him being hungry. Besides, she had never owned a pet before and there was an unexpected pleasure in putting the food in front of him and watching Oren wolf it down with such gusto.

She was just turning away to prepare her own dinner when Oren stiffened suddenly, the hairs on his back standing on end, and she heard a sound coming from the back of the cottage. It was an insistent scratching noise, accompanied by the faint sound of whining. Puzzled, Poppy walked through the large airy greenhouse extension to the door that led out into the rear garden. She opened it and found a scruffy little black terrier sitting on the doorstep.

"*Ruff!*" He looked up at her, wagging his tail eagerly.

"Hello, Einstein—what are *you* doing here as well?" Poppy asked.

"*Ruff! Ruff!*" the little dog replied. Then he lifted a paw and gave a hopeful whine.

"Oh, all right... come in," said Poppy with a smile, stepping back from the doorway.

The little dog scampered in and made unerringly for the kitchen, where he sat down in front of the pantry door and looked up at her again with another hopeful whine.

"Cheeky monkey! How did you know—?" Shaking her head and laughing, Poppy opened the pantry and rummaged around until she found the carton of dog biscuits.

"Now, don't get any ideas," she said to Einstein as she hunted for a bowl. "This just happened to be on sale—like the box last week—and I just happened to be walking down the pet aisle at the supermarket..."

The dog gave her a bright-eyed look, which told her that she was fooling nobody, then shoved his face into the bowl and began gobbling the biscuits. Poppy watched him with a smile, then suddenly remembered Oren. The ginger tom and the terrier were old foes, with regular skirmishes whenever they met in the gardens of Hollyhock Cottage—which happened to be sandwiched between their respective homes. Most of the time, Oren won, although this didn't seem to deter Einstein. In typical terrier fashion, he was convinced that if he just kept trying, he would win next time, and so he hurled himself into battle with fresh fervour every time he saw the cat.

Thankfully, today, he seemed too engrossed in eating. Poppy glanced warily at the other side of the kitchen. Oren had hissed and puffed up to twice his size when the terrier entered the room, and now he sat on the counter, glaring at the dog and growling feline rude words under his breath. But it didn't look like he was planning to hurl himself at Einstein any time soon, so Poppy relaxed and turned to the pantry once more, this time to think about her own dinner.

As she prepared her meal, her thoughts returned to the mystery of Valerie Winkle's death. Try as she might, she just couldn't get John Smitheringale out of her mind. She thought of the day she had seen him in Oxford and the furtive way he had behaved. What had he been doing? Who had he been visiting? She was chagrined now that she had been so distracted by meeting Bertie that she had never gone to take a closer look at those names under the intercom in the end. *The next time I'm in Oxford...* she promised herself.

But in the meantime, the question was—did she say anything to Suzanne Whittaker about her suspicions? It felt churlish, somehow, to snitch on her own client, and yet at the same time, if he *could* have been the murderer, wasn't it her duty to let the police know? Especially as she felt somehow partly responsible for Valerie's death. It was silly, she knew—there was probably nothing that she could have done differently that would have made a difference, but still, she couldn't quite shake off the feelings of guilt.

Poppy placed her plate on the wooden table in the kitchen and sat down in one of the seats, staring unseeingly at the food in front of her. She was well aware that she disliked John and she was afraid that her negative feelings towards him might be making her biased. *Would I suspect him if I liked him better? Still, whether I like him or not doesn't change the fact that I overheard him threatening Valerie during their argument*, she thought, recalling the way John had shaken his fist at the woman.

And it also didn't change the fact that he had been absent from the house during the time when the dead woman's tea could have been poisoned. Just because he *said* he had gone into the village didn't really mean that it was true—had anyone actually seen him in the village?

Plus, the man was a cardiologist, so surely he would have a very good knowledge of the chemicals which could mimic a heart attack? The gap in the hedge worked both ways. It would have been so easy for him to slip over to Valerie's house and doctor her cup of tea, then slip back unnoticed. Or maybe he hadn't even tried to hide. Maybe he had gone over on the pretext of apologising for his recent temper and used that as an excuse to slip something into Valerie's cup when she wasn't looking...

Poppy pulled herself out of her thoughts as she realised that her food was getting cold. It was silly speculating like this. The police might have already confirmed that an eyewitness saw John in the village that morning, which would mean that he couldn't have been at Valerie's house poisoning the tea. Whatever her feelings of guilt, she was better spending her time and energy on her fledgling business, she reminded herself. As soon as she finished dinner, she would go to the greenhouse extension at the back of the cottage and sow her new batch of seeds.

She had just finished her meal and was rising from the table when she noticed strange lights coming through one of the windows. That window faced the other side of the cottage—the opposite to Nick's house—and had a view of the crumbling stone wall which separated Hollyhock Cottage from Bertie's property. Twilight had fallen now, and from her position she could just make out the roof of the old inventor's house through the trees.

"What's your master doing, Einstein?" she asked the terrier, who had finished his biscuits and settled down by the table.

The little dog looked up at her and cocked his head, giving a soft whine. Oren—who had settled on the windowsill to wash himself—paused in his licking to shoot the dog a dirty look. Then he turned his head to gaze out of the window as well. Poppy was about to rise and go over for a closer look when a loud *boom* shook the air and the windows rattled suddenly from the force of an explosion. Poppy gasped and rushed to the window, with Einstein at her heels, barking madly. She could see smoke billowing up from the house next door.

Was Bertie's house on fire?

CHAPTER EIGHT

Poppy rushed out of the cottage and through the garden, making for the section of the wall between her property and Bertie's where one of the stones had come loose, leaving a large gap that Einstein used as his personal doggie door. She stooped low to crawl through, then paused in confusion as she straightened up on the other side. She had expected to find half the house up in flames but, to her surprise, it looked completely fine, every brick and roof tile intact. There was smoke, though, coming out of the windows on the far side—the windows that looked into the sitting room, from what she remembered of the layout.

"*Ruff! Ruff-ruff!*" barked Einstein, who had accompanied her through the hole in the wall. He took off around the corner of the house and Poppy followed him to the back door, which was slightly ajar. No doubt, this was how the dog had got out earlier. She pushed it open and stuck her head in, calling:

"Bertie?"

There was no answer, although she could hear a commotion of voices coming from the front of the house. Puzzled, she stepped in and wandered down the hallway, past the kitchen and bedrooms, and arrived at the sitting room door. The air in the room was hazy with smoke and she stared at the slightly surreal scene in front of her.

A group of middle-aged men sat in chairs arranged in a semicircle, all facing one side of the room where a table had been set up with test tubes, a Bunsen burner, volumetric flasks, and other laboratory equipment. The men all seemed to be dressed in a ubiquitous uniform of navy blazers with brass buttons and carefully pressed beige chinos. They were also all sporting faces black with soot and smoke, and looked more than a little shell-shocked as they sat staring at the old man in the white lab coat who was holding a tangle of wires in one hand and an albino rat in the other.

"Hmm... yes... well, a bit more explosive power than I expected, but on the whole, quite a success, wouldn't you say?" said Bertie, beaming at everyone.

"A success...? A success...?" spluttered one of the men, getting up from his chair and taking a pristine white handkerchief from his pocket to wipe his face. "Dr Noble, you nearly blew us all up!"

"I thought you said it was *safe*," said another man, struggling to rearrange his comb-over. "You said it would be a hazard-free method of repelling rats."

"Yes, you said you were showing us a revolutionary new form of pest control," said a third man indignantly. "I'm certainly not investing in that… that time bomb!"

"Gentlemen… gentlemen…!" said a tall, distinguished-looking, grey-haired man who had been sitting in the front row. He rose from his chair and faced the others, holding his hands up in a placating manner. "I'm sure it was all an accident and Dr Noble will have a very good explanation for what happened and why it's very unlikely to happen again." He turned and looked at Bertie expectantly.

"Oh, no, it's supposed to explode, Mr Fothergill," Bertie said happily. "Although perhaps not *quite* so loudly nor with so much smoke… Of course, the device does rely primarily on ultrasonic waves, but I thought having an actual explosion would increase its effectiveness as a pest repellent. Hmm… but now I see that it may not be as ideal as I thought. Perhaps it needs a bit more testing," he conceded. "This is just a prototype after all… I know! I can remove the explosive element and we can try it again."

Several men looked alarmed and began backing

away.

"Goodness gracious—is that the time?" one exclaimed.

"Er... Must be off. Wife doesn't like it if I'm out too late..." said another.

A third man clapped a hand to his head. "Blimey! I've just remembered, I need to... er... change the battery in my TV remote—"

"I'll come and help you!" cried the man next to him.

There was a stampede for the front door, and within minutes the room was empty except for the distinguished-looking man in the front row. Bertie looked at him with delight. "Ah, Mr Fothergill, I'm so glad you can stay. I'll just—"

"Er... actually..." The man fingered his collar nervously and began edging towards the door. "It's very kind of you to offer to demonstrate your invention again, Dr Noble, but—"

"Not at all, not at all—it's my pleasure. And I'm honoured the president of the association is willing to spend more time considering my work; it's obvious that you're in touch with your feminine side and—"

"I... I beg your pardon!" Fothergill spluttered, going very red in the face and adjusting his trouser belt.

"Oh, that was not an insult," said Bertie earnestly. "I simply meant that the fact you are keen to learn more about my invention shows that you have a more evolved, open-minded way of thinking, which is a result of feminine leanings. You see, there was a study published in *Current Anthropology* that curated the opinions of several academics at US universities, and it postulated that the significant evolution of humankind was due to the 'feminisation' of early man."

"Oh... er... right," said Fothergill, looking confused and relieved at the same time. He cleared his throat. "But I really mustn't take up any more of your time, Dr Noble... I'm sure you will want some peace and quiet while you check your calculations so... er... I'll leave you to it now... Goodnight!"

And he scurried out as fast as his polished brogues could carry him. Poppy felt a bit sorry for Bertie, standing there rather forlornly, still holding the rat and tangle of wires. Hurriedly pinning a bright smile to her face, she stepped out of the doorway and said:

"Hi, Bertie!"

The old inventor turned around and blinked at her owlishly from behind his spectacles. "Ah! Poppy—how delightful to see you, my dear! I'm afraid you missed my demonstration. I was just showing the members of the Oxfordshire Entrepreneurs Association my new invention—"

"Yeah, actually, I heard the explosion—that's why I came over."

"Hmm... hmm... a slight miscalculation, that was all... I just need to recalibrate the scales... Now, where did I put my—"

"*Rrrr-ruff!*" Einstein dashed forwards and launched himself at the rat in Bertie's hand, which began emitting shrill squeaks and struggling to get free.

"Now, stop that, Einstein—bad boy!" Bertie scolded, holding his hand up high to keep it out of the terrier's reach. "You know you're not allowed to chase Celsius or Fahrenheit." He shooed the terrier out of the room and shut the door, then took the rat over to a large cage in the corner.

Poppy followed him and watched as he gently placed the rodent into a pet hammock where another rat was curled up sleeping. He gave it a treat and a pat on the head, then shut and latched the cage door.

"Have you heard the news, Bertie? About Valerie Winkle's murder?" Poppy asked.

It would have been a stupid question to ask anyone else; there was probably not a soul left in the village now who didn't know about the murder—well, not a soul except for Bertie. The eccentric inventor lived in a world of his own and since he rarely went out into the village to socialise, he often didn't know what was happening in the local community.

"Eh?" Bertie frowned. "Who?"

"Valerie Winkle. She's—she was—one of the residents of the village. She lived next door to the Smitheringales, who are my new clients."

"Ah yes... the woman who was poisoned... I saw it on the evening news..." said Bertie vaguely.

"I was there when she became ill. It was awful." Poppy shuddered at the memory. "She was fine one minute and then, all of a sudden, she started staggering around and having trouble breathing. I thought she was having a heart attack, you know—she kept clutching her heart—but the police are sure that it was poison."

"Was she trembling? Did she complain about tingling in her fingers?"

"I... I'm not sure. She was mumbling but it was a bit unclear—yes, she did seem to be shaking and twitching in a weird way, I suppose."

"Were her pupils dilated?"

Poppy frowned. "I couldn't see, really. I wasn't close enough and she was staggering around—"

"Ah yes... you said... yes, lack of coordination is characteristic—"

"Characteristic of what?"

"It is a common symptom of alkaloid poisoning."

"Alkaloid?"

"Yes, I wouldn't be surprised if that was what she was killed with," said Bertie, nodding sagely. "Alkaloids have very powerful cardiotoxic, neurotoxic, and gastrointestinal-hepatic effects. They're a compound found in plants," he added at Poppy's blank look.

"You mean they're plant poisons?"

"Well, not all alkaloids are poisonous. Some of

them have important medicinal uses—like morphine and codeine, for example, which are used for pain relief, and curare, you know, which was used to treat malaria. And in many cases, even if they are poisonous, small amounts won't harm you. You ingest alkaloids every time you have your morning coffee, you know, my dear."

"What? There's poison in my coffee?" said Poppy, startled.

"Not poison, exactly, but caffeine is an alkaloid. That's why coffee wakes you up—you see? It's a stimulant, and in large doses it can cause vomiting, convulsions, irregular heartbeats, even death."

Poppy frowned. "So could Valerie have died from drinking too much coffee?"

Bertie looked doubtful. "In theory, yes, I suppose... but in practice, that would be very hard to achieve as you would need to drink copious amounts since there wouldn't be enough caffeine in a normal cup of coffee for a lethal dose. Of course, people *have* died from an overdose of caffeine, but they are usually caused by caffeine pills or caffeine energy drinks, which have very high concentrations and a lot of sugar to mask the bitter flavour. In fact, most alkaloids are very bitter."

"Oh..." said Poppy, thinking of Valerie's cup of tea and wondering how the woman wouldn't have noticed the bitter taste, if an alkaloid poison had been added.

Bertie continued earnestly, "But you know, it

needn't have been caffeine, my dear. There are many other plant alkaloids which are far more toxic, and some, like strychnine and aconitine, can be absorbed across the skin, or even—as in the case of strychnine—inhaled as a powder! Then there is coniine, from poison hemlock, which causes progressive paralysis and death, atropine from deadly nightshade, which leads to delirium... and even nicotine is lethal if administered in concentrated doses in its pure form. They're all plant alkaloids."

"I think I'm going to get nightmares," said Poppy, laughing wryly. "I'll be too terrified to touch any plant in the garden after this!"

"Oh, I wouldn't worry, my dear. Most plants are quite safe if you don't put them in your mouth. In fact, many of the common plants in most English gardens are poisonous. Things like delphiniums, foxgloves, hydrangeas, rhododendrons—"

"Wait—did you say delphiniums?" said Poppy, jerking upright.

"Yes, all parts of a delphinium contain poisonous alkaloids."

"And does it cause the same symptoms? Like vomiting and heart problems—"

Bertie nodded. "Oh yes. Nausea, vomiting, muscular spasms, respiratory collapse, and cardiac arrest... I had a colleague in the United States who did extensive studies into delphinium poisoning. They're called larkspur over there, you know, and they cause a lot of cattle poisoning in places like Colorado and Wyoming. Dr Howell was trying to determine the effectiveness of treating poisoned animals with cholinergic drugs but I don't think he had much success." He shook his head sadly.

Poppy stared at him, her mind racing. Was it a coincidence that Prunella Shaw—a woman with good reason to hate Valerie Winkle—should be an expert grower of delphiniums?

CHAPTER NINE

Poppy arrived at the Smitheringales' early the next day, eager to get back to work. She smiled with pride when she walked into the back garden and saw the flower bed that she'd planted. Well, half planted. She walked around it, admiring it from various angles, and felt incredibly pleased with herself. *Why did I ever think gardening was difficult?* she thought, grinning and feeling slightly smug. Maybe the villagers were right: she *was* a Lancaster after all, and perhaps she had inherited a natural talent from her grandmother.

It was an unusually hot day—even for midsummer—and the sun beat down relentlessly from a cloudless sky. Poppy was soon drenched in sweat as she dug holes and heaved pots about. The plants looked like they were suffering too; in fact—

she cast a worried eye over the bed—the ones she'd planted yesterday were beginning to droop visibly, their leaves curling and wilting. *Maybe they're just taking time to settle in*, she thought.

Still, despite the heat, she made good progress, putting most of the remaining potted plants into the ground before she decided to call it a day. As Poppy walked back through the village, she suddenly had an idea; she took a slight detour and arrived in the lane behind the church. It was not hard to find the house—you could see the tall spires of flowers spilling out of the garden from the end of the lane—and she paused at last in front of the cottage surrounded by a garden full of delphiniums. They were magnificent: tall, majestic columns of ruffled florets in every shade of blue, pink, white, and purple, which towered over her head.

There was a woman in the garden, crouched at the base of one plant. She wore gardening gloves and a professional-looking gardening apron, and was carefully trimming yellowed and dead leaves. She looked to be in her fifties, with iron-grey hair framing a thin, shrewd face, and a brisk, capable manner. She looked up suspiciously as Poppy approached and rose to her feet.

"Hello..." Poppy gave her a hesitant smile. "I hope you don't mind but I just had to come over and admire your garden. These are the most beautiful delphiniums I've ever seen!"

Her face softened. "Thank you. They're not at

their best this year, but they're not bad." She looked at Poppy more intently. "You seem familiar... Have I seen you around the village?"

"Yes, probably. I moved here recently. I... um... I inherited Hollyhock Cottage—"

"Oh, of course! You're Mary Lancaster's granddaughter," said the woman. "I'm Prunella Shaw. I knew your grandmother, you know. Fantastic gardener. Grew very good delphiniums too." She nodded approvingly. Then she looked at Poppy curiously. "Never realised that she had a granddaughter, though. You never came to visit Mary when she was alive?"

"My mum was estranged from her family," said Poppy awkwardly. "I didn't know... She never talked about them as I was growing up. I never even knew that my grandmother lived here until the letter from the solicitor arrived, telling me that I had inherited the estate."

Prunella raised her eyebrows. "That must have been quite a surprise! What did your mother say?"

"She passed away a year ago, actually, so she never knew."

"Oh! I'm sorry. What about your father? Is he more inclined to mend fences and reconcile with the family?"

Poppy hesitated. She hated it when people started asking about her background. "Er... well... actually... um... my mum brought me up herself."

Prunella's eyes were gleaming with curiosity now.

"Oh, I see... so... did your parents separate when you were a baby?"

Poppy shook her head, her cheeks flushing as she wondered how to answer. She always dreaded this moment in a conversation, when the subject of her father came up.

"Um... no, not exactly," she said.

"Not exactly? You mean—"

"So, how long have you been growing delphiniums?" Poppy asked brightly.

Thankfully, Prunella was easily diverted onto her favourite subject. "Oh, for years. They were always my favourite flower. I'm even trying my hand at breeding now... And you?" Prunella deftly turned the conversation back to her. "I heard a rumour that you're planning to continue your grandmother's business?"

"It's not a rumour—it's true," said Poppy, grinning. "I'm going to reopen Hollyhock Cottage Garden Nursery! I've just planted a batch of seeds and I'm tidying up the garden at the moment—but I should be finished in a week or so. And then I just need to get some pretty bunting to decorate the outside of the cottage and some balloons and print up a few signs, maybe even some labels for the plants, which I could colour-coordinate with the pots—"

"Whoa... whoa...!" Prunella burst out laughing. "You *are* joking, aren't you?"

"No, I'm serious... why?"

Prunella gave another incredulous laugh. "My dear, don't you know how long it takes seedlings to mature and reach a decent size? It's late in the season now—we're heading into the end of July—and most perennials you sow now will need to grow on; they won't be ready for sale until next spring! So what are you going to sell while you're waiting for them to grow?"

"Oh." Poppy was taken aback. "I... I didn't know... I thought I could just plant the seeds and—"

"You *could* try some quick-flowering annuals, like cornflowers—although even there, you really want to get the seeds in the soil by June, because it'll take six weeks to see any blooms. So you're probably too late even for those, especially if you're unlucky and we get an early frost..." She paused thoughtfully. "I suppose you could start some cuttings, although even those will take time—"

"Cuttings?" said Poppy blankly.

Prunella sighed and gave her a pitying look. "You're not your grandmother, are you?"

Poppy flushed, ducking her head with embarrassment. "I... no, I'm a complete beginner."

The older woman looked at her silently for a moment, then she said in a brisk tone, "Chin up. We all had to start somewhere. There's no shame in admitting you don't know something—as long as you're willing to learn. And experience is the best teacher, as they say." She turned to gesture to her own garden. "Look at me—I started knowing nothing about delphiniums, and now I'm probably the top grower in the county."

"Yes, I heard that your flowers win top prize at the show every year," said Poppy, smiling.

The woman's face darkened. "I've been fortunate—except for this year."

"Oh? What happened this year?" asked Poppy innocently.

Prunella scowled. "Valerie Winkle decided to interfere and nearly killed all my prize plants. Yes, I know you're not supposed to speak ill of the dead, but that woman was a menace! Always thought she knew everything—especially anything to do with gardening—and was always muscling in where she wasn't wanted."

"Oh, that's awful!" said Poppy. "You must have been devastated. I know I would have been furious if I was in your position."

"Well, I *was* furious," Prunella admitted. "That morning when I came out and saw the state of the plants, I lost it. I wanted to kill her!" Then she seemed to realise what she'd said and added sourly, "But I didn't murder her. Yes, I know what Mrs Peabody is saying... That gabby old bat... She's going around the village, telling everyone that I killed Valerie, isn't she?" Her chin jutted out. "Well, I didn't."

"I suppose if you have an alibi for the morning of her murder, you would be in the clear...?" said

Poppy in a suggestive voice.

"I don't," said Prunella bluntly. "The police came and questioned me—all because of that bloody Peabody woman—and that's what they asked me: where was I during that time? Well, I told them the truth: I was here, adjusting some of the stakes on my Pacific Hybrids, and adding some extra mulch, but there was nobody here with me. So there are no witnesses to corroborate that." She crossed her arms. "But really, if they want to find out who killed Valerie, they're wasting their time questioning me. *I* don't have any secrets I'd kill for."

"What do you mean?" said Poppy in surprise.

"Valerie didn't just stick her nose where she wasn't wanted—she also liked to *spy* on people. And there are people with secrets in this village—secrets that they are desperate to keep hidden." Prunella paused and added, "Maybe even secrets that they're willing to commit murder for."

Poppy stared at her. "You mean... But who would—"

"I'm not a common gossip like Mrs Peabody!" said Prunella, bristling. "I know how to keep my mouth shut and respect other people's privacy. It's up to the police to keep their ears open and figure it out for themselves. Now... if you'll excuse me, I have to get on with some chores."

With that, she bade a curt goodbye and retreated into her house. Poppy stood for a moment, staring blindly at the rows of delphiniums, then she turned and retraced her steps up the lane, making her way slowly back to Hollyhock Cottage. As she walked, she mulled over the recent conversation. What Prunella had said about the challenges of reopening the nursery made her slightly uneasy. She couldn't afford to wait until next spring to start selling plants! She really needed the cottage garden nursery to start operating and bringing in an income within the next few weeks—but how was she going to achieve that when she had nothing to sell?

Then Poppy thought of the flower bed she had just planted at the Smitheringales' and brightened. Maybe she could do more of such jobs! After all, gardening didn't seem to be as hard as she had thought and there were probably many other couples like the Smitheringales—wealthy city-types with country homes in the area, who wanted nice gardens but didn't want to do their own dirty work. Yes, she could get some leaflets printed and offer her services around; maybe she could even take advantage of the local grapevine. After all, news travelled like wildfire in small village settings and word would probably get quickly around—

Poppy frowned suddenly. The thought of the village grapevine made her think of the other half of the conversation with Prunella and what the woman had said about the motive for Valerie Winkle's murder. Could it be true—that Valerie Winkle had been killed in order to silence her? But what secret could be so terrible that one would resort to murder?

And what secret could have been kept in this village in the first place? Poppy wondered sardonically. After living in big cities most of her life, she had been taken aback, when she first moved to Bunnington, at the idiosyncrasies of village life—in particular, at how everyone knew everybody's business. Sometimes it seemed like you couldn't change your brand of toothpaste without the whole village knowing by lunchtime (and having opinions about it too).

So anyone with a secret that most of the villagers didn't know must have something that they really want to hide, thought Poppy grimly. The question was—was it something they were willing to commit murder for?

CHAPTER TEN

There had been no feline shape waiting in the shadows when she returned that evening and Poppy was surprised to find herself missing Oren's company. As she prepared her lonely dinner, she wondered if Nick was home and had fed Oren early, which was probably why the ginger tom hadn't come over demanding food. *It's only cupboard love after all*, she told herself with a cynical smile.

But it seemed that she was wrong, because a familiar, strident voice sounded outside the front door after dinner and, when she opened the door, Oren strolled in, sleek and well fed, with his whiskers freshly groomed. He wandered over to the armchair she had been sitting on and jumped up, making himself comfortable in the dent of the cushion—as if she had been warming the seat especially for him.

"Hey, *I* was sitting there, Oren," said Poppy, glancing at her half-finished mug of tea next to the chair. "Get off. Go and find your own chair."

"*No-o-o-ow,*" said Oren, tucking his paws under his chest.

Poppy exhaled in exasperation and tried to gently shove the cat off the seat. He rolled onto his back and batted playfully at her hands with his paws, obviously thinking it was a great game.

"Ouch! Stop it, Oren—your claws caught me that time... Ow! Stop it, that hurts!"

After several minutes of struggling, Poppy gave up and Oren stretched out luxuriously against the cushion, a smug look on his face.

Grrrr. Poppy was beginning to wonder why she'd thought she missed the cat's company. She contemplated using a cushion to forcibly push Oren off the armchair, but he looked so comfortable that she didn't have the heart to do it. Instead, she glanced at the sagging sofa in the corner, then picked up her mug with a resigned sigh and moved across, telling herself that it wasn't because she was a pushover—no, certainly not—it was actually more comfortable on the two-seater anyway, with space to put her feet up...

She had barely settled down again when there was a knock at the front door. Sighing, Poppy heaved herself up once more and went to answer it. She was surprised to find Nick Forrest standing on the threshold, his eyes smouldering, his mouth set in an angry line and his unruly dark hair wilder than ever, standing up in tufts as if he had yanked at it furiously.

"Is that bloody cat of mine here?" he snarled.

"Oren? Yes, he just came over. Why—"

"I'm going to wring his neck!" growled Nick, stepping inside. "He'd been pestering me all evening, climbing on my keyboard and blocking my screen while I was trying to write. And then I left my study for one moment—*one moment!*—and the bloody cat knocked my coffee all over the laptop! It's completely dead now and I was in the middle of a crucial scene!"

"Oh no..." Poppy put a hand to her mouth. "You haven't lost the whole manuscript, have you?"

Nick made an impatient noise. "No, it's backed up online, although I've probably lost the last scene I was writing... and now I can't even get back on my laptop to rewrite it! *And* I'm going to have to waste tomorrow taking the machine to a computer repair shop in town." He followed her into the sitting room and glared at Oren. "Mangy beast—I should have drowned you as a kitten!"

The ginger tom gave his owner a baleful look, then deliberately turned his back and began languidly washing his face. Nick made a furious noise and started towards the cat, a murderous look in his eyes, and Poppy hastily jumped between them.

"Uh... will you remember that scene you wrote if you wait until after you get your laptop back?" she asked.

"What?" Nick shrugged angrily. "No, of course I won't! I mean, I remember the plot points, of course, but that's not the same as being able to recreate the exact same paragraphs I wrote earlier. That's the bugger of it—when it's going well, the sentences just pop into your head without you even trying. The perfect words all fitting together in the perfect way; the perfect dialogue, exactly as if those characters were speaking it in front of you... But if you don't write it down immediately—if you try to search for it later—it just somehow eludes you. You can't quite remember how you phrased that sentence or wrote that banter... arrggghh!" He clutched his head in his hands, looking like he wanted to tear his hair out.

Poppy watched him askance. At the rate he was going, he would probably be bald by Christmas. "Well, listen—how about if you try to rewrite the scene now?" she suggested.

"What? By hand?" he snapped.

"Oh... you could, I suppose, but I was actually going to offer my own laptop."

He looked surprised. "Your laptop?"

"It's really old and very slow, so it won't be as good as working on yours," Poppy hastened to say. "But if all you need is something to type on..."

"That's all I need," said Nick. "Have you got an

internet connection? I'll be able to access my online copy of the manuscript and just continue where I left off. But are you sure...?"

"Yes, I'm not using it tonight anyway. You can bring it back tomorrow morning—or you're welcome to just use it here, now." Poppy gestured to the back of the cottage. "It's in the kitchen. You could sit in there and write, if you like?"

Nick looked at her broodingly for a moment, then said, "Thanks—I'll take you up on the offer. The sooner I sit down and try to recreate that scene... although it's probably a lost cause now, anyway," he added morosely. "I'm never going to remember how I wrote that dialogue—"

"You might be surprised. Anyway, you won't know until you've tried," said Poppy briskly, feeling like she was dealing with a sulky five-year-old as she hustled him into the kitchen.

A few minutes later, Nick was ensconced at the kitchen table with Poppy's ancient laptop in front of him and a fresh cup of coffee at his elbow. She left him muttering to himself and pounding away at the keyboard, and tiptoed back to the sitting room, making sure to shut the door between the rooms so that Oren couldn't go and sabotage things. Even with the door shut, however, she could hear the furious tapping of the keys and the sound of impatient cursing every so often, accompanied sometimes by groans of anguish or loud sighs of frustration. It sounded like the most tortuous process and she wondered why anyone would want to be a writer.

When the door finally swung open half an hour later, though, she was surprised to see Nick stepping out with a wide grin on his face. He came into the room, his eyes alight with good humour, and even smiled at Oren as he walked past the armchair.

"So... um... did you manage to remember some of the scene?" Poppy asked tentatively.

"Yes, most of it came back! And I even had a new idea for how to write the dialogue, so I tweaked it a bit—I think it's even better now than it was before!" said Nick enthusiastically, rubbing his hands with satisfaction.

Poppy blinked. Despite having known Nick for nearly a month now and having witnessed several of his mood swings, she could still never quite get used to his Jekyll and Hyde transformation. Now he seemed like a completely different man compared to the snarling bear who had turned up on her doorstep. He was smiling, charming, even affable as he sat down next to her on the sofa and began asking how her work was going at the Smitheringales'. Poppy gave him a summary of her progress so far, and what she hoped to accomplish in the next few days, then said casually, "So you and John seem like old friends—have you known each other long?"

"Yes, we met at Oxford. John read Physiology

and I read English. We sort of lost touch after we left uni... then we reconnected again a few years ago."

"Oh... so you were close friends as students then?"

"Fairly close, although we didn't always see eye to eye on certain things. John can be a bit high-handed sometimes," said Nick dryly. "He wasn't so bad when we were students, but since he's got older and his medical practice has taken off and he's become so successful... well, it might have gone to his head slightly."

He paused, then added quickly, as if feeling the need to make an excuse for his friend, "Besides, I remember meeting his parents a couple of times when they came up to Oxford, for matriculation and graduation and stuff like that. They were terrible elitist snobs—you know, the kind that treat all working-class people with contempt. So John was brought up with those values. I mean, he genuinely believes that a real gentleman should never do any 'rough work'."

Poppy thought John sounded like an absolute tosser and she couldn't understand why Nick would want to be his friend, although she didn't say this out loud. Some of it must have shown in her expression, though, because Nick looked defensive and said, "John's not a bad chap—just a bit 'old-fashioned', you could say, in his attitudes."

You mean he's a male chauvinist pig, thought

Poppy, and she could see from the flicker in Nick's eyes that he had read her mind. Still, she had to concede that John Smitheringale being sexist and elitist didn't make him a murderer. Trying a different tack, she asked:

"Have he and Amber been married long?"

"Oh... a couple of years. In fact, I went to their wedding shortly after John and I got back in touch. He'd only been seeing her for about six months—it was a bit of a whirlwind romance."

"That sounds romantic. He certainly seems very protective of her," commented Poppy, adding smoothly, "Poor Amber seems really upset about what happened to Valerie. How's John taking it?"

"He seems all right. He's pretty stoic in general—maybe it comes from being a doctor. They must be used to dealing with death and that sort of thing."

"Yes, but still—it's not the same when it's someone you know, in your personal life, is it? I mean, this was their neighbour... although I got the impression that John didn't like Valerie much?"

Nick looked at her sharply. "What are you getting at?"

"Nothing," said Poppy quickly, but Nick narrowed his eyes at her, the good humour draining from his face.

"Are you suggesting that John might have something to do with Valerie's murder?"

"I... I think he could be a possible suspect," said Poppy, raising her chin. "I know he's your friend, but you've got to consider the possibility. After all, he hated Valerie and I know he threatened her on the morning of her death."

"What? What are you talking about?" demanded Nick.

"When I arrived at the Smitheringales' that morning, John was having a huge argument with Valerie by the gap in the hedge. He was literally shouting in her face. And I distinctly overheard him say to Valerie: *'...don't push me or you'll be sorry!'*"

"People say things like that all the time when they're angry," said Nick scornfully. "It doesn't mean anything."

"Well, he certainly looked like he meant it."

Nick held up his hands. "Look, I admit the chap can be a pompous arse sometimes, but John's not evil. He's a doctor, for heaven's sake—he's taken an oath to save lives, not destroy them!"

"He wouldn't be the first doctor to ignore their oath," Poppy argued. "Loads of serial killers are doctors."

Nick looked at her irritably. "What is your problem? Why have you got it in for John?"

"I haven't!" Poppy protested, her cheeks flushing at the lie. "I just think that he *could* have been involved, that's all. Do you know if the police have questioned him?"

Nick shrugged. "I haven't spoken to Suzanne in the last few days. In any case, I thought the victim was poisoned. How is John supposed to have poisoned her?"

"That's easy. He could have put something in her tea, when she went in mid-morning for a break—"

Nick burst out laughing. "What? Don't be ridiculous! He's not going to just walk into her house, march up to her teacup, and dump poison in it."

"Well, of course, he wouldn't do it like that!" Poppy snapped. "He would probably distract her, and then slip something into her tea when she wasn't looking. Maybe he had a vial or something in his pocket."

Nick sat back, looking amused. "And where did he get the poison from?"

Poppy made an impatient noise. "You said yourself: he's a doctor! He's got access to all sorts of drugs and medications—"

"They keep a tight check on things these days. Doctors can't just waltz in and help themselves to drugs from a stocked cupboard; everything is signed for and there is constant inventory review and even witnesses that need to be present when retrieving the more dangerous drugs."

"How do you know?" Poppy demanded.

Nick folded his arms. "Because I was researching it for one of my books, where I used an opiate as the murder weapon. This isn't like Agatha Christie's day, you know, when you could stroll into the local pharmacy and buy a bottle of arsenic."

Poppy flushed. "Well, Bertie thinks it's likely to

be a plant alkaloid so—"

"I'm not interested in anything Bertram Noble has to say," Nick cut in coldly.

Poppy bristled. "Why not? He's very knowledgeable about lots of things and he's got some brilliant ideas. I know he seems a bit eccentric but lots of geniuses are like that—"

"He's not a genius!" Nick snapped. "He's just a crazy old man, and if you know what's good for you, you'll stay away from him!"

Poppy stared at him in surprise. There was a furious glitter in Nick's dark eyes but, before she could ask more, he got up from the sofa and said stiffly:

"Thanks for the use of your laptop. I really appreciate it. But I think I'd better be getting back now. Come on, Oren..." He bent and scooped up the ginger tom without ceremony.

"*NO-OWWW!*" complained Oren, struggling in Nick's arms, but the crime author held him firm and carried him to the front door.

As he was about to step out, Nick hesitated and looked back at Poppy. He seemed to want to say something. Then he changed his mind and, with a curt "Goodnight", went out of the door and disappeared into the night.

CHAPTER ELEVEN

"If you take a seat, miss, Inspector Whittaker will see you soon."

Poppy sat down in the chair indicated and tried to shake off the feelings of guilt and betrayal. *I had to come*, she told herself. It was her civic duty to report her suspicions. Nick would understand. After all, he used to be a cop himself—CID, in fact—so he knew how important every lead was in a murder inquiry. If *he* had been in charge of the investigation, he would have been grateful for any information she could give, no matter how far-fetched. Still, she had a bad feeling that Nick wouldn't be as understanding as she'd hoped. *Anyway, why should it matter?* she reminded herself crossly. *It's not as if I care about Nick's opinion or his feelings.*

When Suzanne Whittaker sat down opposite Poppy in the interview room ten minutes later and listened to her nervous account, she smiled as she noticed Poppy's hesitation and constant apologies for suspecting John Smitheringale.

"Relax, Poppy—I'm not Nick and I'm not going to bite your head off just because you dare to suspect my friend."

Poppy gave her rueful grin. "How did you know?"

Suzanne tossed her dark hair and laughed. "I used to be Nick's girlfriend, don't forget. And we came up through the ranks together. I know him pretty well. He's very loyal—and he can let his emotions get the better of him. It was actually something that got him in trouble several times with the superiors during his time in the CID. He was a brilliant and dedicated detective—obsessed, even—but much too volatile and emotionally involved in the cases.

"It was probably just as well that his writing career took off when it did and he left the Force," she added with a wry smile. "Being a successful investigator really requires a coldly analytical attitude towards everything, and the ability to consider the worst in everyone—*even* your friends and family."

Like you? Poppy thought, eyeing the elegant woman in front of her. With her cool beauty and quiet authority, Suzanne Whittaker was the epitome of the successful professional woman. Poppy was sure that the detective inspector never had trouble with her emotions getting the better of her.

Suzanne held a hand up, misunderstanding Poppy's expression. "Oh, don't get me wrong—I still trust Nick's instincts above anything. In fact, I often go and ask his opinion when I've got a tough case. He'll sometimes suggest a clever new way to approach things or an angle I hadn't thought of. He's got this sense of creativity, which no one else seems to match. Probably why his books are such bestsellers," she added with a chuckle. "It was a bit of a liability when he was still in the Force, but now it's all safely channelled into the pages of his novels."

She looked down at the folder in front of her and said, her tone changing back to brisk and professional, "Now... back to John Smitheringale. Thank you for coming to see me about him. I really appreciate it, particularly as he has been on our radar."

"You mean—you already suspected him?" said Poppy in surprise.

"Well, perhaps not as a serious suspect, but we do question everyone in the vicinity and check their relationship with the victim."

"Oh! Do you know if anyone saw him in the village that morning?" asked Poppy eagerly. Then she caught herself and gave Suzanne a sheepish look. "Sorry, I didn't mean to be cheeky—it's just that I wondered if he had an alibi."

Suzanne laughed. "Don't worry, you're tame compared to some of the villagers who have been bombarding me with questions. Many of them seem to think that it's the police's duty to provide them with detailed updates on every aspect of the murder investigation! And no, I don't mind telling you: no one saw John Smitheringale in the village that morning."

"But John said he was going into the village to buy something—so surely someone *must* have seen him? It's not a tiny village but it's not huge either, and most of the shops are concentrated around the high street and the village green."

"Well, as a matter of fact, I have confronted John about that. He admitted that he didn't go into the village in the end. He said he changed his mind and went for a walk instead. The Smitheringales' house is situated at the edge of the village and there are several walking paths around that area. He says he wanted to get out into the countryside for some fresh air."

"And did anyone see him out walking?"

Suzanne smiled. "You're quick. No, no one saw him walking either. So it seems that John Smitheringale doesn't have an alibi for a crucial portion of that morning."

Poppy sat back and digested this.

"However... he isn't the only person who may be involved in Valerie Winkle's murder and it would be unwise to focus solely on him," Suzanne reminded her. “We need to keep an open mind and consider any other likely suspects as well.”

“You mean like Prunella Shaw?”

Suzanne raised her eyebrows. “How did you know she’s under suspicion?”

“I think the whole village knows by now,” said Poppy with a laugh. “Mrs Peabody has been telling anyone who would listen. And in fact, Prunella herself told me that you questioned her about her alibi for that morning.”

“Ah... then you’ll know that she has no firm alibi either.”

“Yes. By the way, there’s a way to get from her house to Valerie’s, using the back lanes, rather than walking through the centre of the village,” said Poppy. “I know because I did it myself yesterday when I went to see her after finishing at the Smitheringales’. So she *could* have sneaked over without anyone seeing her, especially if she went very early in the morning, when there were fewer people about.”

“Hmm... well, nobody reported seeing her near Valerie’s cottage—we’ve asked around the village—but that’s good to know. Thanks.” Suzanne made a note in her pad. Then she said: “Apparently Joe Fabbri, the local handyman, was seen knocking on the door of Valerie’s cottage the morning that she died. Do you know him?”

“Oh... I think he does odd jobs for the Smitheringales, like mowing the grass and clipping the hedge."

"Have you met him yourself?"

Poppy shook her head. "I didn't realise that he worked for Valerie too."

"Well, I don't know if he works for her regularly. When I questioned him yesterday, he told me he had just been doing her a favour—he had taken some of her gardening tools away for cleaning and was returning them."

"That's funny—I got the impression that they weren't on friendly terms," said Poppy in surprise. "Amber told me that she'd heard Joe being quite sharp with Valerie when Valerie tried to meddle in his work."

"Hmm..." Suzanne made another note in her pad. "Well, in any case, Joe says she was fine when he saw her that morning."

"She would have been," said Poppy. "She was fine when I saw her—and that was a few hours later."

Suzanne inclined her head. "Yes, and considering the amount of toxin in her system and the type, she must have ingested the poison only a short while before she collapsed. Otherwise, she would have started showing symptoms earlier."

Poppy looked at the detective inspector shyly. "Can I ask what kind of poison it was?"

Suzanne smiled. "Well, it'll probably be mentioned in the press anyway... Yes, I got the results back from the full tox screen. There were lethal levels of aconitine in her system. Aconitine is an alkaloid—a type of toxin produced by plants."

"Oh! Bertie was right!" cried Poppy.

"I'm sorry?"

"Bertie—I mean, Dr Bertram Noble, who lives next door to me—told me that the poison was likely to be a plant alkaloid."

"Hmm... he's very astute," commented Suzanne. "Yes, apparently aconitine comes from the *Aconitum* plant,

"*Aconitum*? I think I've read about that... Isn't it supposed to be one of the deadliest plants in the world?"

Suzanne nodded. "Yes, according to the forensic pathologist, just a tiny amount—like two milligrams—is enough to kill you. In fact, it *has* been used in several poisoning attempts, since the 1800s. There was even a recent murder—in 2009, I think it was—committed by an Indian woman in London, who poisoned her lover with aconitine. She used a toxin from an Indian version of the plant, which she had to fly to India to get, but I understand that the common form is frequently found in gardens all over England. Apparently, the flowers and buds are quite pretty." She made a face, obviously thinking that people had to be mad to have such a dangerous plant in their gardens, no matter how attractive it was.

"If it's found in gardens, then that means it would be easy for anyone to get hold of the poison,"

Poppy said excitedly. "They don't even have to remove the whole plant—they could just pick off a few leaves and buds."

"That's right. Although aconitine is also available in homeopathic preparations and herbal medicines. It's very popular in TCM—Traditional Chinese Medicine," Suzanne explained at Poppy's puzzled look. "In fact, most cases of fatal poisoning recorded come from Asia—in places like Hong Kong, China, and Taiwan—where aconite root is used in herbal remedies."

"People actually eat it on purpose?" said Poppy incredulously.

"Well, apparently aconitine does have some beneficial effects in small doses. The problem is that the safe dosage is so small, it's really easy to get it wrong and overdose. And an overdose can be fatal."

When Poppy walked out of the police station several minutes later, she felt as if a weight had been lifted from her shoulders. Yes, there was still a niggle of guilt and unease at her reporting John Smitheringale, but that was tempered by the knowledge that the police had already been investigating him anyway.

She felt flattered, too, by Suzanne's willingness to discuss the case with her and by the detective inspector's seeming respect for her opinions. It was a such a nice change from her previous job in London, where her boss had constantly mocked her lack of skills and qualifications... Poppy smiled as she felt a rare boost to her self-esteem. She was suddenly very glad that she had decided to come see Suzanne that morning!

CHAPTER TWELVE

Poppy paused outside the police station, wondering whether to head straight back to Bunnington. She was not expected to start work at the Smitheringales' until after lunch so she had a few hours to kill. It was a blisteringly hot day again and, for a moment, she was tempted just to stretch out on a sunny patch of grass somewhere and enjoy the summer weather. But she reminded herself that she couldn't afford to laze around—for one thing, she still hadn't figured out what she was going to do about her garden business. Prunella's laughter at her ignorance yesterday still echoed in her mind and she felt embarrassment fill her again.

Could she really rely on finding enough gardening jobs to tide her over until next spring? But that was nearly ten months away... and autumn was already around the corner. What would happen when winter rolled around? Nobody wanted to spend time out in their gardens in winter; people retreated indoors in the cold, dark months and didn't think about the garden much until spring came again… so who was going to hire her?

Poppy chewed her lip worriedly, fighting the anxiety that was starting to fill her again. Then suddenly she thought of Nell: she had always turned to her old friend for comfort and reassurance, and now she took out her phone and eagerly dialled Nell's number.

"Hello, dear—how nice to hear from you. How are things going in Oxfordshire?" Nell's voice sounded strange—subdued and flat, and completely unlike her usually cheerful self.

Poppy had been about to launch into a litany of her woes, but now she checked herself and asked uncertainly: "Nell? Is something wrong? You sound a bit odd."

"Oh no, everything's fine…" Nell paused, then sighed and said, "Well, actually, everything's *not* fine. I got some bad news this morning. The cleaning franchise I work for has been bought out by another company and they're letting a lot of their cleaners go. I'm out of a job."

"Oh no… Nell—I'm sorry to hear that! But can't you go and work for another cleaning franchise?"

"I've tried contacting some of the other places before and they made it clear that they didn't want me." Nell's voice hardened. "They didn't come out and say so, but I suspect it's because I'm older. Probably thinking I'd be taking sick leave more often or something." She made an indignant sound. "Well, I can tell you, I'm a lot fitter than half these young whippersnappers they employ, who can't even scrub a toilet properly. I've never taken a sick day in my life!"

"What about going... er... freelance?" Poppy suggested. "I mean, couldn't you just clean for people privately?"

Nell sounded doubtful. "I could try... but my company serviced a lot of offices in town. Most businesses used them. Where am I going to find enough independent jobs to replace all those places?" She sighed again. "It's hard for an individual to compete with the big cleaning companies, you know—they have a professional website and a national presence and people know the brand..."

"I'm sure you'll find other jobs," Poppy said. "Perhaps if you advertise—"

"And that's not all," Nell continued. "I found a note from the landlord in the letterbox this morning, telling me that my lease has been terminated."

"*What?* How can he do that? Don't you have a contract?"

Nell sighed. "Yes, but if you can claim that the tenant broke the terms of the contract, you can ask them to leave early. Which is what he's saying. He's bringing up the subletting again and using that as the excuse."

"But I've already left!" cried Poppy. "As soon as he complained—which he shouldn't have anyway, since he himself agreed to our subletting arrangement—but as soon as he said anything, I left the house. I haven't been living there since. Surely he can't be punishing you now, a month later?"

"Poppy, dear, it's just an excuse. The truth is, he needs a quick way to get me to leave and that reason was convenient."

"But why does he need you to leave? You always pay the rent on time, you keep the house in good condition, you never complain when he's slow to repair problems—"

"It's money," said Nell crisply. "I was chatting to Mrs Waltham on the other side of the street and she told me she heard that this area is marked for redevelopment. A big property developer has bought up half the street and is planning to convert the townhouses into luxury flats. We're close to the train station and a short run into the centre of London. This is a prime location. I'm sure what's happened is that they've offered my landlord a tidy sum for his property too. So he wants to kick me out, so that he can sell quickly and pocket the money."

"When do you have to leave?" Poppy asked.

"I've got until the end of the month."

"Well, that's still two weeks away. I'm sure you'll find somewhere else to live by then," said Poppy brightly.

Nell sighed again and said in a tired voice, "It was practically a miracle finding somewhere with such low rent, so close to shops and transport—I don't know how I'm going to do it again, especially at such short notice. And now that I don't have a job, my application will be much weaker—they always give preference to those with stable employment."

Poppy had never heard Nell sound so down and dispirited. Her old landlady always seemed to meet any adversity with a cheerful optimism—it was something that Poppy had found wonderfully comforting, especially in the final days of her mother's illness. To hear Nell sound so hopeless was very unnerving.

Then a thought struck her. "Listen, Nell—I've just had a brilliant idea! You can come and live with me!"

"With *you*?"

"Yes, there's plenty of room in the cottage here. It's not huge but there are two bedrooms, and we were already used to sharing a bathroom. There's not much in the way of mod cons, I admit," Poppy said with a rueful laugh. "I mean, the water is hot but only just, and the bathtub is a relic from the last century; the kitchen is very basic and the stove is ancient... but everything is fully functional."

"Oh, Poppy—that's really sweet of you to offer, but... what about my work?"

"Well, without your job, what's tying you to London? You could come and look for work up here. Oxford itself isn't that far away and it's a small city. There are loads of offices and retail premises there that would need cleaning. Or you might even find a position working for the University. All those colleges and departments... loads of cleaning needed there!"

Her enthusiasm was obviously rubbing off on Nell. Her old friend's voice sounded more cheerful as she said:

"You know, Poppy, maybe you're right... Maybe this is a chance for me to have a fresh start. And I've always fancied moving to the country... But are you sure?" she added anxiously. "I mean, aren't you enjoying having your own space, after all this time? Do you really want to have to share a house again?"

"Don't be silly! I'd love to have you living with me. The cottage has been feeling a bit lonely, to tell you the truth. Besides," Poppy added, chuckling, "you don't realise I have an ulterior motive. If you're living here, then I get to eat your delicious cooking, instead of the pathetic meals that I cobble together."

Nell laughed. "All right. You've convinced me. I'll come... but on one condition: I want to pay you rent."

"What? No, don't be ridiculous—"

Nell's voice was firm. "I'm serious, Poppy. I won't take the accommodation for free. I'll only agree if I pay you rent."

"I... oh, all right. For now," said Poppy, knowing from experience that once Nell got that tone in her voice, it was useless to argue.

"Good." Nell laughed suddenly. "Oh my lordy Lord, it will be a funny reversal—me subletting from you, for a change!"

CHAPTER THIRTEEN

As she ended the call with Nell, Poppy had an idea and, instead of heading back to Bunnington, she hopped on a bus for Oxford. When she arrived, she found the university city busier than ever, the streets packed with tourists eagerly photographing the beautiful architecture and local residents eagerly soaking up the summer sunshine. She alighted at the bus station in Gloucester Green and made her way unerringly to an office unit just around the corner, where she looked up with distaste at the garish red-and-yellow hoarding above the door. It displayed a poster of a middle-aged man in a shiny suit, with a large moustache and a cheesy grin, and the words:

LEACH PROPERTIES LTD.

Everything I touch turns to SOLD!

Poppy stared at the poster and wondered if she should follow her first instincts and avoid this place like the plague. Then she shook away the thought, took a breath, and went in.

The girl at reception looked up with a smile of recognition and said: "Hey—you're the girl with the alstro! How's it doing?"

"Great!" said Poppy, returning her smile. "I've planted it in a spot by my front door and it's always covered in flowers." She glanced towards the inner office and asked. "Um... is Mr Leach in?"

"Yeah, let me call him. This about renting a flat, isn't it?"

"Oh no. Um... I'm actually his cousin," said Poppy.

The girl's eyes rounded. "Ohhh! You're the girl who's inherited Hollyhock Cottage and deprived old Hubert of his rightful inheritance!" she said, chuckling. "He's been banging on and on about that for weeks!"

Poppy flushed. "Yes... well... it was a complete surprise to me too," she said gruffly. She knew that her grandmother changing her will at the last minute wasn't her fault and she shouldn't feel guilty, but she still felt bad all the same.

"Hey, don't stress about it," said the girl with a grin. "Hubert's a stingy old bastard; it'll do him good to have to fork out his own money for things, for a change."

Poppy was a bit startled to hear the girl speaking like this about her own boss. Obviously, Hubert didn't command much respect from his own staff! Before she could reply, however, Hubert Leach flung open the door from the inner office and walked out. He wasn't sporting that cheesy smile, but otherwise he was the spitting image of the poster outside, with his cheap navy suit, loud yellow tie, and greasy moustache.

He saw Poppy and stopped short, a sour look crossing his face. "Cousin Poppy! To what do we owe this pleasure?" he asked sarcastically.

Poppy gave him a hesitant smile. "Uh... hi Hubert... do you have a moment? I just wanted to ask you something."

He turned and gestured to his office with a flourish. "Of course. Anything for my *favourite* cousin."

Poppy winced at the sneering words and preceded Hubert into the office, where she sat down facing the desk whilst Hubert lowered himself back into his leather executive chair. He didn't look particularly welcoming and Poppy wasted no time in getting to the point.

"Hubert, you manage rental properties, don't you? And those need regular cleaning, especially when the tenants leave. Do you use a particular cleaning service?"

"We use a couple of different ones. Why?" asked

Hubert in a bored voice.

"I've got a good friend who's coming to live with me and she's looking for work locally. She's a cleaner. I thought perhaps your cleaning companies might be interested in hiring her? Could you give me the details for the contact person at each place?"

A gleam came into Hubert's eyes. "Well, now... I can do better than that. I could offer your friend a permanent contract cleaning all the rental properties we handle. And this office as well."

Poppy's eyes widened. "Really?"

Hubert gave an expansive smile. "Of course. We are family, after all, and family have to help each other, don't they?" Then he added smoothly, "Of course, in return, I would expect to be able to call in a favour sometime."

Poppy eyed him warily. "I don't have any money to give you, Hubert. I told you, all the capital from the estate is wrapped up in the land and property."

"Oh, I'm not asking for money. My goodness, would I be so crass?" said Hubert with a look of exaggerated horror. "It would only be a trivial thing—a bit of back-scratching in return, eh?"

Poppy regarded him uneasily. All her instincts were telling her to say no; striking a deal with Hubert was a bad idea... but if he could offer Nell a job, it would be a big load off her old friend's mind. Nell had done so much for her—she wanted to try and repay the other woman in some way. Besides,

Poppy reminded herself that, after all, Hubert *was* her cousin—her only family. And she had never had an extended family and didn't know how things worked. Maybe this was what family did for each other...

"Okay," she said.

"Ah! So I have your word?"

Poppy took a deep breath. "I promise."

Five minutes later, Poppy left the real estate agency with a sigh of relief and hoped that she wouldn't regret her promise. She headed towards the north of the city and soon found herself in the now-familiar area around the university science departments. She retraced her steps to the sandwich shop where she had seen John Smitheringale the other day, and walked up to the doorway she had seen him go through. The brass plates beneath the intercom gleamed in the bright midday sun and she had to squint to read the words engraved on them.

Telford & Worthing Accountants... Olympus Training Solutions... X-Group Website Services... Golden Lotus TCM... Bullseye Marketing... i-Spy Studios...

Wait.

Poppy ran her finger back up the row of plates and stopped at the one marked "Golden Lotus TCM". Her interview at the police station that morning came back to her and she heard Suzanne's voice once more in her head:

"Aconitine is also available in homeopathic preparations and herbal medicines. It's very popular in TCM—Traditional Chinese Medicine..."

Poppy drew in a sharp breath. Quickly, she took out her smartphone and did a search for "Golden Lotus TCM" on the internet. After all, "TCM" could have stood for "Tax Consulting Management" or even "Toilet Covers & Mats"... But no. She found it almost instantly in the local business directory. The entry read:

"Golden Lotus TCM is located in Oxford and offers a team of experienced and professional Acupuncture and Traditional Chinese Medicine (TCM) practitioners. Chinese herbal medicine is mainly plant-based and has been used for thousands of years; it has great benefits in general health maintenance and disease prevention. It is based on the concepts of Yin and Yang, and takes a holistic approach to..."

Poppy looked back up at the name on the brass plate and wondered if John Smitheringale was one of Golden Lotus's clients. She couldn't be sure that he had been pressing *their* buzzer that day. There were five other businesses on the list below the intercom. He could just as easily have been visiting the accountants or going to see someone at the recruitment agency... How could she find out which business he had been visiting?

As she was pondering this, the door opened and a woman stepped out. She looked at Poppy enquiringly and held the door with a smile. Without thinking, Poppy thanked the woman and went in. She climbed the stairs to the second floor, where the clinic of Golden Lotus TCM was located, and stepped into a cool reception room. Tinkling Chinese music and a bamboo water feature gave the place a soothing ambience, and the blinds at the windows kept the lighting soft and gentle.

The Chinese lady behind the reception counter looked up and smiled at her. "Hello. Welcome to Gold Lotus... how I can help?"

"Er..." Poppy hesitated. She had come up on an impulse and had no plan, no idea of what to say. "Um... I'm interested in trying some... er... Chinese medicine."

"You have special problem?" the woman asked. "Or you just want tonic for good health?"

"Er..." Then an idea struck her. "Actually, a friend of mine has been using TCM and he told me about this great clinic he'd found. I was really keen to try it myself, but I couldn't remember the name of the clinic. I know it's in Oxford and when I saw your sign downstairs, I thought I'd pop in on the off-chance that you might be the place..." She gave the woman a persuasive look. "I don't suppose you could tell me if my friend is one of your clients? His name is John Smitheringale."

The woman glanced over her shoulder towards

the rear of the clinic, then lowered her voice and said with a conspiratorial smile:

"Not really allow to give client information... but is okay—I look for you." She turned towards her computer and began clicking with her mouse. After a few moments, she said: "Ah ya... Mr Smitheringale come here few time."

"Oh, great," said Poppy. "Thank you—then I'm in the right place." She wished she dared ask what John had come in for, but she knew she would arouse too much suspicion if she asked for confidential information like that.

"You want have consultation now?" the woman asked. She looked intently at Poppy's face. "Ah! Yes, your face look muddy—must have blockage in *qi* channel... You show me tongue?"

"T-tongue?" Poppy stammered.

"Yes, yes, show me..." The woman gestured impatiently towards Poppy's mouth.

Poppy hesitated, then opened her mouth and stuck out her tongue.

"Hmm..." The woman peered at her mouth with disturbing intensity. "Shape no good... thin tongue..."

"Is that bad?" asked Poppy in alarm.

"You have yin deficiency... maybe bad heat in lungs..." The woman looked thoughtful, then asked, "You have stinky discharge from nose?"

"What? No!" said Poppy indignantly.

"Is no shame. Very common." The woman waved

a hand, then she looked at Poppy's face again. "Ah-ya... you have deep line between eyebrow... This mean liver problem from frequent anger..." She eyed Poppy in a critical fashion. "You have bad temper?"

"Me? No! I'm... I'm a very calm person," said Poppy. Between the thin tongue, stinky discharge, and bad temper, she was beginning to feel really aggrieved now. "Look... um, actually, you know what? I'm in a bit of a rush so I think I'm going to have to come back another day."

"Okay, I make appointment for you?" The woman held her hands poised above the keyboard. "Your name, please?"

"Uh... well, er... I think I'd better go home and check my diary first... I can't seem to remember my schedule now for the coming week... but... um... I'll ring and make an appointment once I get home... thanks very much... Goodbye!"

Giving the woman a hasty wave, Poppy hurried out of the clinic and escaped down the stairs. She breathed a sigh of relief as she stepped back out into the street. Then she looked thoughtfully back at the brass plaque next to the intercom, engraved with the TCM clinic's name. John Smitheringale was a Western-trained doctor. Would he really go to a TCM practitioner, with their strange beliefs in blocked *qi*, excess heat, and yin and yang, for his own health? She *could* think of something that he *would* go to a TCM practitioner for, though... to obtain an aconite root mixture for use in poisoning his meddling neighbour.

CHAPTER FOURTEEN

Poppy was surprised to see a strange car parked in the cul-de-sac outside Hollyhock Cottage when she arrived home. It was a sleek grey BMW and she wondered for a moment if someone had come to visit Nick Forrest. But when she pushed open the garden gate, she discovered that the visitor was actually for her. A slim woman with dark hair in a stylish bob was waiting by the front door of the cottage, and Poppy realised that it was Christine Inglewood.

"Hello!" she said in surprise. "I'm sorry—have you been waiting long?"

"Not at all," said Christine with a frosty smile. "And I have been enjoying your garden. I remember you saying it had been badly neglected but—" she glanced around, "—it looks pretty good to me.

You're doing a great job restoring it."

"Thank you!" said Poppy, flushing with pleasure. "I'm sure it doesn't look anything like when my grandmother had it, but I hope it will get there eventually."

"And have you thought about renovating the house at all?" asked Christine quickly. She looked back at the cottage, surveying the exterior. "It's long overdue for a makeover. There's great potential here, though—the bones are solid and you could do so much to expand and modernise, while keeping the period character of the place."

Poppy eyed her warily. Had Christine come to scout for business?

"I'd love to renovate the cottage at some point but... um... I haven't got any funds at the moment," she said in a guarded tone. "I don't know how much Amber has told you, but I inherited this place from my grandmother and I'm now trying to resurrect her garden nursery business. I haven't got any capital at all so it's going to be tough for a while."

Christine made a sympathetic face. "Yes, Amber had told me a bit about your situation. In fact, it's why I'm here—she was describing your place to me and it sounded like a property that was just begging for a makeover! So I had to come over to take a look." She paused, then said impulsively, "Listen, I have an idea... as you know, I have a list of landscapers that I often liaise with and recommend to my clients. People who are renovating and redecorating often think of redoing their gardens as well. I know you're just starting out and may need a bit of help with promotion. I'd be happy to pass your details along to any clients who might be looking for someone to help them in their garden. Especially smaller jobs, which might not require the attentions of a full-scale landscaping company."

"Oh!" Poppy felt ashamed of her earlier assumption about the woman's motives. Her experience with Hubert Leach had made her cynical and she'd forgotten that not everyone shared her cousin's self-serving attitude. "Thank you! That's... that's really nice of you."

Christine gave another of her trademark chilly smiles. "Well, I can remember when I was starting out myself and how grateful I was for every client recommendation. It's nice to be in a position to pay it forward. Besides..." She looked back at the cottage and her smile widened a fraction. "I'm hoping that, in return, you might keep me in mind when you finally come to renovate this cottage. I would love to take on a project like this—it would be a real creative challenge."

"Okay, you're on!" said Poppy, returning her smile. "If—when I can finally afford to renovate the cottage, you'll be the first person I call." Then, feeling more cordial towards her visitor, she gestured to the cottage door and asked: "Would you like to come in for a cup of tea?"

"Thank you. That would be lovely."

When Poppy returned to the sitting room with two mugs, she found Christine sitting in the armchair and surveying the room with an interior designer's eye.

"This has great potential to be a wonderfully comfortable house. Are you here by yourself?" she asked.

"Yes... although actually, I have a friend in London who will be moving here soon to live with me."

Christine raised her eyebrows. "Oh... and your family? Are they nearby?"

Poppy hesitated. "My mother passed away last year."

"I'm sorry... and your father?"

"Er... I didn't... I don't really know him."

Christine's eyes flickered with interest. "Oh?"

Poppy felt the familiar irritation and she said, rather curtly, "No, my parents were not divorced, they didn't separate when I was a baby—I just don't know him, okay?"

"I didn't mean to pry," said Christine hurriedly. "It's just that I grew up without a father too."

"Oh." Poppy flushed, ashamed now of her brusque reply. "Oh... I... I'm sorry. I didn't mean... it's just that in the village, everyone keeps asking—"

"Yes, I can imagine. People are so gossipy, aren't they? Those living in cities might be more blasé about different lifestyles, but out here, in these small villages... the minute they find out that your family doesn't have a conventional background, they want to know every sordid detail." Christine grimaced. "I used to hate it when I was a little girl. When my dad left us, I used to dread going out and being asked where he was or what had happened to him."

"Yes! I know what you mean," cried Poppy, looking at Christine with new eyes. "That's exactly how I felt—still feel most of the time. I'm so tempted sometimes to make up a nice, safe backstory to use, like saying my mother was a happy housewife and my father was a doctor—"

Christine gave a humourless laugh. "Not that safe. My dad *was* a doctor—that didn't stop him leaving me and my mother."

"Oh... um..." Poppy floundered, then grinned, trying to lighten the mood again. "A dentist then?"

Christine laughed, more genuinely this time, and started to reply, but she was interrupted by a familiar plaintive voice outside the front door.

"*N-ow! N-OW!*"

"What on earth is that?" asked Christine, startled.

"Oh, that's Oren. He's Nick Forrest's cat," said Poppy, getting up to let the ginger tom in. A minute later, Oren strolled into the room and stopped short at the sight of Christine sitting in the armchair. *His* armchair.

He scowled, his whiskers quivering. "*H-ow? H-oow?*" he demanded.

Poppy patted the sofa cushion next to her and called him to come over, but he ignored her. Instead, he jumped up onto the arm of the armchair and glared at Christine. She looked back at him with an expression of distaste.

"*Ahem*... does he want something?" she asked at last, after several seconds of them eyeballing each other.

Poppy grinned. "I think he doesn't like you sitting in his chair. He probably wants you to get off."

"*N-ow*," Oren added, looking pointedly at Christine.

The interior designer looked nonplussed. "Well... I'm not getting up for a cat! He can go and sit somewhere else."

Oren flicked his tail angrily, then deliberately climbed into Christine's lap, turning and shoving his furry bum into her face. His tail whipped across her forehead, ruffling the sleek fringe of her perfect bob. Christine reeled back and spluttered in outrage.

"Oren!" Poppy cried, embarrassed and horrified. "Oren—get off!"

"*No-o-o-ow!*" said Oren, lashing his tail.

Poppy sprang up to grab him and the ginger tom jumped away, knocking Christine's Louis Vuitton handbag off its perch on the other arm of the chair. The bag tipped over, spilling its contents everywhere. Christine made an exclamation of annoyance and got up to retrieve the bag. As soon as she rose from her seat, Oren dived into the armchair and made himself comfortable, a self-satisfied expression on his orange face.

"I'm sorry," Poppy groaned as she bent to help Christine collect the spilled items. "He can get a bit stroppy if he doesn't get his own way."

"That's why I hate cats," muttered Christine, shooting the ginger tom a dirty look. "Sly, spiteful creatures!"

"Oh, he's not that bad," said Poppy, feeling obliged to defend Oren. "He's just a bit wilful and naughty sometimes. But he's also good fun at other times and very affectionate too."

"Mmm..." Christine didn't look convinced.

She restored everything to her handbag and straightened again. Poppy wondered if she was going to insist on returning to the armchair but, to her relief, the interior designer hesitated, then turned and sat down on the sofa instead.

"It's only because I don't want to get cat hairs on my clothes," she hastened to say, picking fastidiously at the fabric of her skirt.

Poppy laughed to herself. That might have been true, but she had a feeling that Oren had scored a victory. The ginger tom was washing himself in a leisurely fashion now, his loud purring filling the room. Christine gave him another look of distaste, then deliberately turned her back on him and said to Poppy:

"I actually haven't seen you since that morning when we were having tea—just before Valerie died." Christine gave a shudder. "That must have been a horrible shock for you, seeing her poisoned like that."

"Yes, it wasn't very pleasant. But I've stopped having nightmares about it now," said Poppy.

"And I hear that you're quite friendly with the inspector who's investigating the murder...?" said Christine, looking curiously at Poppy. "Has she told you anything? Do the police know how Valerie was poisoned?"

Poppy hid a smile. So... for all her chilly reserve and elegant manners, Christine Inglewood was as much of a gossip as Mrs Peabody!

"They think it was something she ate or drank—maybe when she went in for morning tea."

"Ah... Do the police suspect anybody in particular?"

Poppy started to answer, then impulsively asked a question of her own. "Christine—what do you think of John?"

"John?"

"Yes. John Smitheringale."

Christine's expression closed. "Well... he's just a client. I don't know him very well. I understand that he's a good doctor, with a very successful private practice in London," she said stiffly

"I heard that you two don't get along?"

"Where did you hear that?" Christine looked

surprised.

"Amber told me. She said that you and John didn't agree on a lot of the plans during the renovation... and that now, he often makes an excuse and leaves, when you go to visit them."

Christine's expression soured. "Men like John want to have their cake and eat it too," she said bitterly. "He doesn't like it when successful, strong women stand up to him."

"So you two have had some rows?"

Christine gave a tight nod.

"Well, when you were arguing..." Poppy hesitated, then plunged on. "Was there ever a time when you felt... threatened? Like, did John ever get physically violent?"

Christine tossed her head back and laughed. "With *me*? I'm not Amber," she said contemptuously. Then she added, "You're thinking he might be a suspect in Valerie's murder, aren't you?"

"Yes," Poppy admitted. "He seemed to really dislike her."

"Well, that might be true, but I think you're barking up the wrong tree. Whatever else I might think about him, I know John's not a murderer. He's a doctor and he takes his medical oath very seriously."

It was the same thing that Nick had said and Poppy felt irrationally annoyed at the thought of the crime writer being right after all.

"Do the police have John down as a suspect for the murder?" Christine asked. "I thought a woman called Prunella Shaw was the top suspect. The ladies from the local church committee were all talking about it when I popped into the village post office shop earlier. Something about revenge for ruined delphiniums?" Christine looked puzzled.

"Yeah, Prunella Shaw lives in the village; she grows prize delphiniums and Valerie sabotaged her plants and ruined her chances of winning this year's show." Poppy frowned. "It seems like such a lame motive for murder, though."

Christine shrugged. "People can do all sorts of impulsive things when they're angry." She rose from the sofa. "Now, I'd better get going. I've got a meeting in Oxford after lunch."

Poppy glanced at her watch and was startled to see that it was well past noon. "Oh my goodness, yes, me too! I mean, not a meeting but I need to go—I'm due at the Smitheringales' after lunch as well. Thanks so much again for coming," she added warmly as she rose to see Christine out.

When she returned to the sitting room, she found that Oren had left the armchair and was trying to crawl underneath it.

"Oren? What is it?" Poppy dropped down on her knees next to him.

He was groping for something with his paw and, when she bent to look, she caught the gleam of gold. She squinted. It looked like a tube of lipstick.

Yes, in fact, she could see a faint "Estée Lauder" etched on the lid. It must have fallen out of Christine's handbag and rolled under the armchair. Hastily, she reached out and grabbed the lipstick before Oren could snag it in his claws. After losing out in the Battle of the Chair, somehow she didn't think Christine would feel very forgiving if Oren broke her lipstick too.

As she pulled the lipstick out, a length of ribbon, which was tangled around it, came as well. The ribbon was attached to a small square tag—the kind that often accompanied gift-wrap—with the words "*To Christine*" and a short scrawled message on the back.

"*N-ow!*" said Oren, reaching up and trying to catch the ribbon with his claws.

"Hey, Oren... stop!" laughed Poppy, lifting the lipstick out of his reach.

She took it into the kitchen and placed it on the counter; she would take it with her to the Smitheringales' and ask Amber to return it to Christine. Then she made herself a sandwich and wolfed it down, before grabbing her things and heading out.

CHAPTER FIFTEEN

The Smitheringales' house seemed to be empty when Poppy arrived and she guessed that Amber must have gone out. In any case, it didn't matter as she could get access to the back garden without going through the house, and she set off happily down the path that took her around the side, to the back of the property. But when she arrived at the flower bed where she had been working yesterday, she felt her heart give a sickening lurch.

The plants looked awful. They were all drooping badly, their stems limp and wilting. The leaves, which should have been glossy-green and healthy, were dull and shrivelled, with several turning yellow and brown. All the rose blooms were faded, their petals curled and burnt at the edge.

"Oh my God... what happened?" Poppy cried in a

horrified whisper as she walked around the bed, staring at the plants. They had been fine yesterday! How could they have gone downhill so fast? She noticed that the batch she had planted on the first day looked the worst and she suddenly had a guilty memory of seeing those same plants looking a bit unhappy yesterday. She had brushed it off, telling herself that they would be fine once they settled in—but now she squirmed and wished she hadn't been so dismissive.

But what should she do? She looked around and spied the garden hose. Rushing over, she grabbed it, turned on the tap, and hurried back to the flower bed where she drenched the plants and flooded the soil around them.

After several minutes, Poppy turned the water off and stood back, holding the dripping hose and staring in horror at the scene of carnage before her. The beautiful flower bed that she had been so proud of yesterday was now a muddy quagmire, with puddles of water everywhere and bits of wet soil splattering everything. The plants hung sodden and dripping, looking even more bedraggled, and several had toppled over under the force of the hose.

Oh no... no, no... no, no...! The panicked refrain kept running around her head in circles. *What am I going to do? What am I going to do?*

A sound from the house made Poppy jerk her head around and her heart fly into her mouth. Had Amber come back home? What was her client going to say if she came out and saw this disaster? All the beautiful roses and plants she had bought and entrusted to Poppy... now shrivelled and dying. The Smitheringales would fire her instantly—and this was the only job she had!

Poppy looked wildly around and her eyes lit on the small shed at the side of the house. She ran over and yanked the door open. Unlike the cobweb-ridden and rat-infested shed at the back of Hollyhock Cottage, this one looked like something from a show home. Everything was neatly stacked and shelved, or hanging on hooks strategically placed on the wall—Poppy half expected things to have little labels with their brand and price attached! In fact, the various bits of equipment, supplies, and garden paraphernalia looked so colour-coordinated that she wondered if Christine Inglewood had had a hand in organising them.

Still, at least it made hunting for things a lot easier, and Poppy immediately spied the collection of wooden stakes neatly arranged against the wall. She grabbed several, then turned and scanned the rest of the contents in the shed... *Aha!* One of the shelves held several large garden waste bags, in green canvas fabric. She grabbed a few of those as well and rushed back out to the garden. There, she set to work, ripping the seams on the bags and spreading them out so that they each unfolded into a long rectangular panel of canvas fabric. Then she attached them to the wooden stakes, which she arranged around the flower bed, so that when she was finished, they formed a sort of screen around the plants.

At last, Poppy stood back, panting, and checked her handiwork. It looked strange and unsightly, but at least it hid the plants from view and would buy her a bit of time until she figured out what to do. She would just have to think of an excuse to tell Amber...

Another sound from the house made her turn around and, through the glass of the French doors, she saw someone moving about the living room. Taking a deep breath, Poppy walked up to the house and was surprised when, instead of Amber, she found John at the door.

"Yes? Oh hi, Poppy." John looked at her without much enthusiasm.

"Hi... is Amber around?"

"She's just popped into the village. Can I help?"

"Oh... er... um..." Poppy hesitated. She had never found John's supercilious manner easy to deal with and now, with him looking slightly impatient, it seemed even more awkward to suddenly say: *"DO NOT LOOK BEHIND THE SCREEN!"* Instead, she fumbled around for some conversation to ease into first and was relieved when she remembered that she had the perfect excuse.

"Actually, I wanted to give these to Amber," she said, pulling the lipstick and tangle of ribbon and gift tag out of her pocket. "They're Christine's. They fell out of her handbag when she was visiting me."

He took the items, glancing at them curiously, and Poppy took advantage of his preoccupation to add casually:

"Oh, by the way—can you also tell Amber that I've erected a screen around the new flower bed. This is... um... to protect the plants. Tell her she mustn't touch the screen or... er... peek behind it. Just for a few days..." Poppy hesitated, as he didn't reply. "Okay?"

He looked up from the items, startled. "Hmm... what? Oh, sorry. Yes, of course... I'll tell Amber when she gets back."

"Thanks." Poppy wondered if she ought to make an effort to be sociable. After all, John *was* her client too. But her unease with him made it difficult to think of any pleasant small talk and, after another awkward silence, she bade him goodbye and went out again.

Back beside the flower bed, she stared despairingly at the dying plants, wondering what to do. She couldn't hide them from Amber forever—she *had to* tell her client the truth—but when she thought of having to admit her huge failure and seeing Amber's face, she couldn't bear it.

Maybe... maybe... if the plants die, I can just buy replacements and replant them, without telling Amber? she thought wildly. But what if she couldn't find the exact same plants as the dead ones? Plus replacing all those roses and other plants would probably cost a fortune—they were all advanced specimens and Poppy had visited enough garden centres to know that large, mature plants were expensive. She would be losing a big chunk of her income from this job just to replace the plants.

Besides... another horrifying thought struck her: what if she spent all that money replacing them—and they died again? After all, she had no idea why the plants had gone downhill this time and no idea how to prevent it happening again. She realised suddenly how incredibly naïve it had been of her to think that she could just take on a job like this, when she had so little experience of plants and gardening. She cringed now as she thought of how smug she had been yesterday, preening herself over her "success" with the flower bed.

At last, Poppy decided that standing there agonising wasn't helping anyone. She couldn't do anything else in the garden now, so she might as well finish early and go home. Perhaps if she had a chance to calm down, have a cup of tea, and think clearly, she could come up with a plan.

She packed up for the day and left, relieved that Amber still hadn't returned and she could slink away unseen. When she got back to Hollyhock Cottage, Poppy dived into her grandmother's books and rifled frantically through the pages, searching desperately for some kind of solution or even just an explanation for the plants' condition. But while the hardbacks, with their beautiful, glossy photographs, were ideal for browsing and ogling different plant varieties, they didn't offer much in the way of practical gardening advice.

In desperation, Poppy fired up her ancient laptop and started scouring the internet for answers. But her search left her more confused than ever. There seemed to be a multitude of different reasons for the same plant symptoms! Yellowing leaves could be caused by too little water… or too *much* water… or compacted soil… or fungi in the soil… or root knot nematodes… or too little light… or nutrient deficiencies… or it could all just be normal ageing!

Aaarrrgghhh!

After a few hours of bewildered reading, Poppy leaned her elbows on the table and clutched her head in her hands. She felt as if her brain was going to explode and she was still no wiser as to why the Smitheringales' plants had suddenly gone downhill. Without a definite cause, she had no idea how to fix things.

I need some fresh air, she thought, stumbling to her feet.

Outside in the garden, Poppy took several deep breaths and felt slightly better. She caught sight of the hand hoe she had been using a couple of days ago, abandoned by the side of the path, and decided to return to her weeding for a bit. At least, she might feel like she was achieving something.

Still, after plucking half-heartedly at various

tufts for an hour or so, Poppy gave up and returned to the house, where she drifted morosely from room to room, searching for something to distract herself. She was relieved when dusk drew in at last and she tried to find comfort in the now-familiar routine of letting Oren in, feeding him a tin of cat food, making her own dinner, and then settling down in the sitting room with a cup of tea, whilst the ginger tom lounged in the armchair and washed himself with leisurely precision.

A part of her wanted to ring Nell and pour out her troubles to her old friend again but something stopped her from picking up the phone. Perhaps it was a form of silly pride, but if she talked to Nell, Poppy knew that she would have to confess the whole sorry affair, including her own gross incompetence. She had wanted Nell to be proud of her; she had wanted to amaze everyone, to show the villagers that she was worthy of the Lancaster name and its legendary talent for gardening... Instead, she would have to reveal how dreadfully she had failed—and she just couldn't bear it.

Poppy decided to have an early night. Didn't everybody say things always looked better in the morning? Maybe after a good night's sleep, she would wake up refreshed and with solutions to all her problems. She picked up a protesting Oren from the armchair and put him gently outside, then she switched off all the lights and went to bed. But she found that her pillow didn't offer much comfort either. In fact, after tossing and turning for half an hour, she sat up again with a sigh.

The window in her bedroom was open and the curtains lifted as a breeze wafted in, bringing with it the scent of roses and verbena. She breathed deeply, and then—on an impulse—she got out of bed, dressed quickly, and went outside. Perhaps a walk through the scented herbs and flowers would soothe her restlessness and calm her mind, enough to let her fall asleep.

Poppy stepped into the garden and stood for a moment, enjoying the ambience. The day had been very hot and the night was still warm, but whereas the heat had been oppressive during the day, now the air was soft and balmy. Leaves rustled and murmured in the breeze. The garden was nothing more than a mass of dark shapes, and yet Poppy got a sense that it was alive—shifting, breathing, swaying around her.

She stepped off the main path and took the small trail that led to the stone wall which adjoined Nick's property. There was an old marble bench there, she recalled, underneath the crab apple tree. It would be a great place to sit for a while and enjoy the night atmosphere of the garden.

As she walked along the path, carefully stepping over some overgrown bushes and trailing vines that she hadn't had time to trim back yet, she found her mind once more drifting back to the dying plants at the Smitheringales'. *No, stop it. Stop brooding. It's not helpful.* She forced her thoughts away, groping around for something to latch her mind on to, and for some reason, Christine Inglewood's lipstick came to mind—or rather, the ribbon and gift tag that she had found with it. Something about those things was nagging her...

Poppy frowned as she stared into the darkness, trying to remember the scrawled message on the tag. "*To Christine*" it had said... and then something like: *"you are the care for my addition"...*

Well, that made no sense! Still, personal notes often contained phrases that sounded like gibberish to the outsider but had special meaning to the recipient. Also, the handwriting had been appalling so she might have read it wrong...

Poppy stopped suddenly on the path.

Yes, she *had* read it wrong! It wasn't "*addition*"... it was "*addiction"!*

She frowned again. The message still didn't make sense, though. "*You are the care for my addiction*"... what on earth did that mean? It would have made more sense if it read "*You care for my addiction*"—but she was *sure* the first two words in the message were "*You are...*"

Then it struck her. Of course! She had misread that too... it wasn't "care"—it was "cure"! So the message actually read: "*To Christine—you are the cure for my addiction.*"

Well, that made a bit more sense, but it was still an odd message. Why would you call someone the cure for your addiction? It sounded like something a lover would say...

Then Poppy thought of something: on the first day she had arrived at the Smitheringales', she had nearly walked in on John and Valerie having a heated argument across the hedge. She had overheard John warning Valerie not to push him or she would be sorry, and the murdered woman had replied: *"Oh, I think not. I think* you *are the one who's likely to be sorry, Dr Smitheringale. After all, you have to think of your addiction, hmm?"*

Poppy felt a thrill of excitement. Surely it couldn't be a coincidence? Those words had meant something to John—and Valerie had known it. She had uttered them with the supreme confidence of someone who had a hold over another. And John—despite obviously being furious—had stopped short and backed down. In fact, he had almost looked... scared.

Blackmail. The word popped suddenly into Poppy's mind.

Valerie had had some kind of hold over John and Poppy was sure it was something connected to Christine—who happened to have a gift tag which also referred to an "addiction". Had John given a present to Christine, with that gift tag attached? But that didn't make sense... John *hated* Christine. Didn't he?

Poppy had almost reached the bench under the crabapple tree, but her steps slowed to a stop as the truth hit her at last. She couldn't believe that she had been so stupid. She couldn't believe that she hadn't seen it earlier.

She gasped out loud. "Oh my God! They're having an affair!"

CHAPTER SIXTEEN

"I beg your pardon?"

Poppy jumped and realised that there was someone already sitting on the marble bench under the tree. He stood up and stepped out of the shadows, and she saw that it was Nick Forrest.

"What are you doing there?" she demanded. "Are you spying on me?"

"What? Why on earth would I want to spy on you?" Nick scowled.

"Then what are you doing skulking there?"

"I wasn't skulking! I was thinking."

"*Thinking?*"

"Yeah, I was trying to figure out a snag in my bloody plot."

"Oh... your book." Poppy remembered belatedly that Nick had told her, when she first arrived, that he often came to walk through the cottage garden when he was stuck in his writing. Something about the rambling, untamed nature of the place seemed to help creative thinking, and her grandmother had invited him to visit whenever he liked.

"You told me it was all right if I continued coming over sometimes," Nick reminded her. "Are you changing your mind?"

"No… it's fine. I'd forgotten. Sorry."

Nick looked at her curiously. "What are *you* doing out here at this time of the night?"

"I couldn't sleep, so I thought a walk might help, and then I was thinking about Valerie's murder and—oh Nick!" She clutched his arm impulsively. "I've got proof that John is the murderer!"

His brows drew together. "What?"

"It's true! I've just figured it out—his motive, I mean. I thought it was too far-fetched that he would murder Valerie just because she was an annoying neighbour… but it's not so far-fetched if he murdered her to stop her blackmailing him!"

"Blackmail?" Instead of being impressed, Nick looked sceptical. "What would Valerie be blackmailing him about?"

"About his affair with Christine Inglewood."

Nick burst out laughing. "John doesn't even like Christine."

"That's what he wants everyone to think!" said Poppy. "And he's succeeded so far. But it's all a front—a cover—so that nobody would suspect that the two of them are having an affair."

"How do you know that they *are*?"

Poppy told him about the argument she had overheard and the cryptic remark that Valerie had made—which matched the scrawled message on the gift tag.

"That's not proof that they're having an affair," said Nick.

"Oh, come *on*!" said Poppy impatiently. "What else do you need? It's just too much of a coincidence. In fact, now that I know, I can see so many little clues—like Amber telling me that John used to come up from London every week to check on the progress of the renovation, and Christine being at the house almost every day... What a handy excuse for the two of them to enjoy regular illicit trysts!"

She paused and added, "Christine also made a comment this morning when she came to see me, which didn't quite make sense. She said 'men like John want to have their cake and eat it too'—it seemed a slightly strange thing to say in the context of our conversation. We were talking about John being a male chauvinist who felt threatened by strong women. Now it makes complete sense, if Christine knew that John was playing the Perfect Husband and also had a mistress on the side. She must have been having a private laugh at my expense!"

"It still could all be coincidence..." Nick said,

although he sounded less certain now.

Poppy ignored him and pressed on. “You should have seen John’s face today when I handed him the lipstick with the ribbon and gift tag. Amber wasn’t there so I asked him to give them to her, to return to Christine. He was horrified when he saw the gift tag—which must be from a present he’d given Christine—but he was also massively relieved that he had intercepted it before Amber saw it. He must have felt like he’d dodged a bullet. That’s why he looked so odd.” She shook her head with reluctant admiration. “He really had us all fooled.”

Nick was silent for a moment, then he said, “Okay… even if what you say is true—John is having an affair with Christine—it’s still a big leap to him murdering Valerie Winkle.”

“No, it’s not! Valerie found out about the affair and started blackmailing John. In fact, Prunella Shaw told me that Valerie was always spying on people around the village and—” Poppy gave a little gasp. “I’ve just remembered! When I was talking to Prunella, she actually said that there are people in the village who might be willing to commit murder to stop others finding out their secrets. Those were almost her exact words.”

“Well, that may be true, but that doesn’t mean John is one of them,” Nick pointed out.

“It all fits!” Poppy insisted. “I even saw John in Oxford, going to visit a TCM clinic—a traditional Chinese medicine place,” she explained.

"So?"

"So—Suzanne told me that the poison which killed Valerie was a plant alkaloid called aconitine and one of the places you can get it nowadays is from TCM herbal remedies. I'm telling you—it all fits! He was acting really furtive too, when I saw him. It was on the afternoon of the first day I met the Smitheringales... which was the day before Valerie died. It's all too much of a coincidence! I mean, why else would John be visiting a TCM clinic?"

"I don't know—to get some acupuncture?" said Nick with an impatient shrug. "You can't make assumptions like that just because you saw a man walk into a clinic—he could have gone in there for all sorts of reasons."

"He's a Western-trained doctor! Why would he be using Chinese medicine?"

"Loads of Western doctors still believe in alternative therapies."

"Okay, so then why was he acting so furtive?"

"Maybe he wasn't and *you* imagined it."

"I did *not* imagine it," said Poppy hotly. "I'm sure he—"

"And I'll tell you something: I *know* John and he just would not murder anyone! It's not in his nature."

"Did you think it was in his nature to have an affair?" Poppy challenged.

"Yeah, actually... I'm not surprised," said Nick,

looking slightly uncomfortable. "John is a bit of a womaniser. Even at college... well, I remember once he had two girls on the go and neither of them knew about the other. Look, I'm not saying that I condone his behaviour," he added, seeing Poppy's disgusted expression. "But shagging around and cheating on your wife is very different to committing murder."

"You're just biased because he's your friend and you don't want to believe anything negative about him!" Poppy snapped.

"And *you're* biased because you've taken against him for some reason and you're determined to believe the worst of him!" Nick shot back.

The two of them glared at each other, breathing hard. Finally, after a moment, Nick said in a slightly calmer voice:

"Look, I think you're on the right track with Valerie blackmailing someone. That's one of the most common motives for murder. Fear will drive people to do something drastic and there's nothing like the fear of a secret coming out. But—" he raised his voice as Poppy started to speak, "—I really don't believe John is one of those people. You don't know him like I do. He values his professional reputation above anything else—it's tied to his ego and his sense of self-esteem. If he's arrested for murder, it would mean the end of his medical career. Even if he managed to hire the best lawyers and was found not guilty, or served only a brief sentence and got out early on some technicality, the whole episode would still tarnish his professional reputation forever. He'd probably be struck off the medical register and lose his licence—but even if he wasn't, I doubt patients would want to see a doctor who has been a murder suspect." Nick shook his head. "It just isn't worth it. Especially over something as trivial as his wife finding out that he's having an affair!"

"That's hardly trivial," protested Poppy. "A lot of men would do anything to prevent their wives from finding out and possibly ruining their marriage."

"Yes, well... John isn't a lot of men," said Nick with a rueful smile. "I'm not sure he would think that an affair would 'ruin his marriage'. If anything, he probably thinks that it's a man's due to play around and it's his wife's place to accept things—as long as he provides a comfortable home for her and gives her his name to use and his ring to put on her finger."

"What? Don't be ridiculous! This isn't the 1950s!"

"No, but some men still have quite old-fashioned views when it comes to women and marriage. You said yourself that John was a male chauvinist. I'd have to agree with you there."

"Well, in that case, if he's so arrogant and sure of himself, he would never think that he'd get caught," Poppy argued, still not willing to give up on her theory. "He wouldn't see murder as a risk, since he fully expected to get away with it."

Nick made an irritable noise. "Why can't you

accept that Valerie might have been blackmailing *someone else*? Why does it have to be John?"

"Okay—who?"

"I don't know!" Nick threw up his hands. "There are any number of people in the village who might have secrets that they want to keep hidden. If Valerie had been going around prying where she shouldn't, it wouldn't have been surprising that she stumbled into something that got her killed..."

"In this village?" Poppy said doubtfully. "This sleepy little place with the Saxon church and the pretty village green and the do-gooders like Mrs Peabody?"

"Don't be fooled by appearances," said Nick. "Even the most genteel places have dark currents lurking under the surface. In fact, I would argue that the more respectable a person is, the more sordid a secret he or she is likely to have."

"But... it would be like looking for a needle in a haystack," said Poppy, shaking her head. "How could we possibly know who Valerie might have been blackmailing?"

"I'll bet she's the type to keep a record somewhere—maybe copies of her letters or even details of her victims. There's bound to be evidence somewhere in her cottage." Nick snapped his fingers. "In fact, let's go and have a look now."

"W-what?" Poppy stared at him, sure that she had heard wrong.

"It's dark now, nobody will be there—it's a great

opportunity to search the place."

"But... but the police have already searched the place and found nothing."

Nick waved a hand. "That doesn't mean anything. I know from my CID days that sometimes these searches can be quite cursory, especially when manpower is down and they're not sure what to look for. Besides, some of the boys in the Force can be a bit... well, unimaginative when it comes to detective work. They tend to only look in the obvious places."

"And you think you can do better?"

Nick gave her a boyish grin. "Why don't you try me?"

"Me? Wait—you want me to come too?"

"What's the matter? Scared?" He looked amused.

"No, of course not!" said Poppy quickly. "I just... I don't think—"

"Come on!"

CHAPTER SEVENTEEN

Nick strode down the path towards the front gate and out of the garden. Poppy had to run to keep up with his long legs.

"Wait—! Nick, we can't... What if we get caught?"

"We'll make sure that we don't."

"That's not an answer! I'm not... Wait...!"

Poppy ran after him as he jogged silently across the village, and caught up just as he slowed to a stop in the lane leading to Valerie's and the Smitheringales' houses. She was slightly annoyed to see that while she was panting and gasping, and had a stitch in her side, Nick seemed to be barely out of breath. For a man who supposedly spent his days typing at a desk, he was remarkably fit!

He paused by a tree in the lane and scanned the area. The Smitheringales' house came first and beyond that was Valerie's smaller cottage. Lights were on in the former and Poppy could hear the faint sound of music and voices coming from a TV, whilst all was dark in the latter.

Nick hurried past the Smitheringales' house and approached the front of Valerie's property carefully, keeping to the shadows and moving with a tense, wiry grace, like a large cat. Poppy tried to copy him, although she had a bad feeling that her version was closer to bovine than feline. She joined him in the bushes next to the front door and eyed the blue-and-white police tape which was stretched across the doorway. She had forgotten about that.

"Nick... we can't—Look!" She pointed to the tape. "We can't go in! Not only are we entering a private residence without permission, but we'd also be entering a crime scene. It's against the rules."

He raised an eyebrow. "And you never break the rules?"

Without waiting for her to answer, he slipped out of the shadows, ran lightly up the front steps, and bent over the front door. Poppy hurried after him.

"What are you doing?" she hissed, watching him in horror.

"Picking the lock—what does it look like?" said Nick. "Look, if you're going to stand there, can you stop gasping like an outraged fishwife and do something useful, like keep a lookout for anyone coming?"

Poppy spluttered angrily, but Nick had already

bent over the lock again. Giving the back of his head a dirty look, she turned and began surveying the area. Behind her, she could hear Nick muttering and cursing under his breath, then finally he made a sound of triumph and the door swung open. He grinned at her, his dark eyes gleaming with excitement, then ducked under the tape and disappeared into the house. After a moment's hesitation and with another hasty look over her shoulder, Poppy ducked under the tape as well and followed him.

It took her eyes a few moments to acclimatise to the dim interior of the house. They didn't dare switch on any lights, but the light from the streetlamps outside slanted in through the windows and lit the rooms just enough to see by. Poppy followed Nick from room to room, marvelling at how neat and organised everything was. Books were carefully shelved and arranged in order of height, newspapers and magazines were neatly folded and stacked in a magazine holder, hats, umbrellas, tote bags, and keys were hung on rows of hooks by the front door, cushions were plumped and placed at perfect right angles to the sofa seats, chairs were tucked under the dining table with perfect alignment. Here and there was evidence of a police search—papers rifled, a few books pushed askew, furniture that had obviously been shifted—but overall, the place had been left as the murdered woman had it.

"Wow..." said Poppy, looking around. "If there's anything here, Valerie's probably got it in a filing cabinet, marked 'Blackmail Information'," she said, chuckling.

"That's not a bad idea," said Nick thoughtfully.

"I was joking," said Poppy, rolling her eyes. "You don't seriously think—"

"The labelled filing cabinet? No. But I was talking more about the idea of hiding something in plain sight. Ever heard of 'The Purloined Letter'?"

Poppy frowned. "It's a short story by Edgar Allan Poe, isn't it?"

"Yes—it's a classic and it's considered to be one of the first detective stories. It's about a stolen letter that the police couldn't find, despite thoroughly searching a hotel room from top to bottom—but an amateur detective found it with no problem, because he realised that the letter was disguised with some other everyday junk, in a card rack in full view of everyone in the room. The police never thought of looking there because they assumed that the blackmailer would use a more elaborate hiding place."

"You think Valerie's done the same thing?" said Poppy, looking around again at the obsessively neat room.

Nick nodded. "I think it's possible that she's hidden it in an everyday place, out in the open—rather than in a secret drawer or under the floorboards somewhere."

"But surely, if you're going to do that, you'd need some kind of 'mess' to hide the items?" Poppy gestured around the room. "This place is so tidy, there's nothing to use to conceal other things."

"Not all tidy," commented Nick, nodding at a large basket in the corner.

It was a knitting basket, filled with balls of wool and knitting needles, as well as a few pairs of socks, a half-finished scarf, and various tangled knots of yarn. Poppy felt her pulse quicken with excitement. Nick was right. The basket stood out as the only "messy" thing in the room. She hurried across and dropped to her knees beside it, then rummaged through it eagerly.

"Anything?" Nick hovered over her.

Poppy sighed and shook her head, rising to her feet again. "No, nothing."

She was about to turn away when she caught sight of something in the bookcase nearby. On one of the shelves was a large shoebox, filled with several brown paper envelopes. She went over for a closer look, pulling the shoebox out and tilting her head to read the writing on the surface of the envelopes.

"What are they?" Nick came up behind her.

Poppy squinted at the spidery writing on the first envelope. It read: "*Antirrhinum majus*". She flipped to the next envelope, which said: "*Aquilegia vulgaris*". The next said: "*Calendula officinalis*" ...and the next one: "*Dianthus barbatus*".

"Oh... they're seed packets," she said. "They're in alphabetical order." She lifted one of the envelopes and shook it, and they heard the faint sound of seeds rattling. She put it back and ran a hand down the row of envelopes, flipping them over like dominoes. "There's nothing here..." she said in disappointment, starting to push the shoebox back into the shelf compartment.

"Wait—" Nick reached over her shoulder to fish out one of the envelopes. He read the name written on the envelope out loud. "*Harpocrates semperflorens*... is that an unusual plant name?"

"Mmm ... '*semperflorens*' is quite a common species name, I think. You know Latin plant names are binomial, right?" said Poppy, eager to show off her newly acquired knowledge. "There are always two words in the name. The first is the genus name—that's the family the plant belongs in—and the second is the species name, which usually describes that particular plant in some way. Well, '*semperflorens*' means ever-flowering and so it's used for a lot of plants in different families, that flower a lot. The ones I've read about are *Begonia semperflorens, Iberis semperflorens, Rosa semperflorens*—"

"Okay, but what about the *Harpocrates* part?" asked Nick impatiently.

Poppy frowned. "*Harpocrates*... I've never heard of that genus name. But that doesn't necessarily mean anything. It might just be an obscure plant family. I haven't learned the whole of my grandmother's plant encyclopaedia by heart, you know... yet."

"But all of these other seeds are for common plants, is that right?" asked Nick.

"Yes. *Antirrhinum* is snapdragons and *Aquilegia* is columbines... yes, they're all common garden flowers. That's why I recognised them. Why?"

"Well, then, why would Valerie have one envelope with an obscure plant genus on it?"

Poppy shrugged. "I don't know. Does it matter? Why are you so interested?"

"I'm interested because Harpocrates is the Greek god of silence and secrets."

Poppy stared at him. Then she reached for the envelope and shook it gently. There was the familiar rattle of seeds but it sounded slightly muffled. Quickly, she turned the envelope over and pulled the flap open. Tucked inside, next to several dark-brown seed pods, were several pieces of folded paper—the thin, translucent kind traditionally used for letters. She pulled them out and unfolded them, holding them up to the light from the windows.

"Bingo..." said Nick softly.

The spidery writing that was on the envelopes—Valerie's writing—also covered the sheets of paper. There were several sections crossed out and rewritten, and it was obvious that these were rough drafts of letters she had sent. Poppy skimmed the sentences: *"...I know your dirty little secret—I've seen you through your windows... how you love your black teddy... wouldn't want everyone in the village to know, I'm sure... don't worry, your secret is safe with me—for a price...*"

Nick gave a low whistle. "She was blackmailing someone, all right." He rifled through the pages. "And it looks like she's been doing it for some time."

"It could be John...?" said Poppy. "He'd be wealthy enough to pay these blackmail demands."

But even as she said it, she could feel doubt creeping into her voice. She wondered if Nick might be right, and whether she was fixating on John Smitheringale because of blind prejudice. After all, those letters could have been directed at anyone. There was nothing to indicate that Valerie was threatening to reveal an extra-marital affair.

She cleared her throat. "Maybe you're—"

"Shhh!" Nick caught her wrist suddenly in a hard grip. "Listen! What's that—?"

A bright light flashed suddenly outside. Poppy gasped and would have frozen on the spot like a frightened rabbit, in full view of the windows, if Nick hadn't ducked instantly sideways and yanked her with him. He slithered along the wall, keeping to the shadows and making for the front door. They reached the entrance hall just as they heard someone fumbling at the door.

"Quick! In here!"

Nick opened the coat cupboard, shoved her inside, then stepped in after her and jerked the door closed behind him—a second before the front door opened.

Poppy held her breath, her heart pounding. The coat cupboard was tiny and pitch black inside, aside from a sliver of light coming from the crack beside the door. She was wedged against Nick's chest, with his arm hard around her, and the heavy folds of Valerie's wool jackets and raincoats crammed around her head. The fabric of Nick's cotton T-shirt felt cool against her cheek, and she could smell the faint fragrance of a spicy male cologne, mingled with the clean scent of soap. She had been held by a man before, of course, but it hadn't felt like this...

She started to pull back, but Nick's arms tightened and she felt his voice in her ear.

"Shh... don't move."

Outside, footsteps sounded in the entrance hall. A torch played over the walls, then turned, directing the beam of light down the hallway. There was a muttered oath, then the person moved down the hall and into the sitting room. Nick's arm loosened enough to allow Poppy to shift closer to the door and press her eye to the crack. They could hear the sounds of rummaging, of cupboards being opened, furniture being moved and papers being shuffled. Finally, she saw the dark figure come out of the sitting room and pause uncertainly in the hallway. The light from the torch swung around again, briefly illuminating the person's face. It was a man.

Poppy caught a glimpse of tanned, leathery skin, grey hair pulled back from the face, and dark eyes crinkled at the corners.

There came another sound from outside the house and, even as she stiffened, she saw the dark figure freeze as well. His torch went out and he stood still, as if listening, in the darkness. Poppy hardly dared breathe and she could feel the muscles of Nick's body tensing next to hers. Suddenly the dark figure darted towards the door. He opened it a crack, as if checking that the coast was clear, and then, after a moment, slipped out and shut the door behind him.

Poppy blew out a sigh of relief and relaxed. Then she realised with horror that she had sagged against Nick's chest and was leaning a bit too comfortably into his arms. Hastily, she jerked back, putting as much distance between them as she could in the cramped space.

"Um... I think he's gone... I mean, he *could* come back but I don't think so... and we'd better get out while we can..." she stammered.

He didn't say anything, although she caught a glint of amusement in his eyes as he let her go and turned to open the cupboard door. They tumbled out of the coat cupboard and, a few minutes later, they slipped quietly out of the house in their turn.

"Did you see who it was?" asked Nick, still keeping his voice low as they walked slowly away from the front door.

"It was a man, but I didn't recognise him. Older, I think. Grey hair. Tanned skin."

"Hmm." Nick frowned. "He was obviously searching for something, although I don't think he found whatever it was he was looking for."

"Well, it has to be something underhanded, otherwise why wouldn't he just come in the daytime? Do you think he was searching for those letters?" Then Poppy gasped. "Nick! The letters! We just left them open like that by the shoebox—"

"Relax. I shoved them back in the envelope before we left the sitting room. They should still be in the shoebox with the other seed packets."

Poppy gave him a look of reluctant admiration. "You're pretty cool under pressure. Is that something you learned during your time in the CID?"

Nick laughed under his breath. "I don't know if Suzanne would agree. She always thinks I don't stay cool and unemotional enough." He glanced back at the darkened house. "Anyway, we got what we came for—and I think it's high time I saw you back to your house, Miss Lancaster. Wouldn't want to be accused of keeping you out too late, eh?"

Poppy was surprised to feel a twinge of regret. She didn't want to admit it, but she had enjoyed herself more than she'd expected. She'd never done anything like this before and there was something exhilarating about taking risks and breaking the rules. Not that she would ever admit it to Nick, of course.

Still, as they began making their way back across the village, she had the strangest feeling that the crime writer had guessed her thoughts. And oddly enough, for once, she didn't seem to mind.

CHAPTER EIGHTEEN

"My goodness, Poppy—you're early today," Amber Smitheringale called as she leaned out of the French doors to look into the garden. She was wearing a pretty floral dressing gown, with her hair tousled and her cheeks slightly flushed, and had obviously just got out of bed.

Poppy whirled guiltily around. She had come over as early as she had dared, hoping to see some kind of improvement in the plants, but they had looked as bad as yesterday. Now she said, in as nonchalant a tone as she could manage: "Uh… hi, Amber. I'm sorry—did I wake you up?"

"No, no… I was awake. Just lounging in bed." Amber smiled. Her gaze drifted to the canvas screen erected around the plants and she said curiously, "John told me that you'd put something around the plants... to protect them, he said?"

Poppy took a deep breath. Now was the time to tell Amber the truth. Everyone made mistakes and she was sure the other girl would be understanding, especially if she offered to replace the plants at her own expense.

"Um..." Poppy hesitated. Then, before she could stop herself, she babbled: "Yes, that's right. You know, like... er, windbreaks. When plants first go in the ground, they're very susceptible to wind damage and... er... toppling over, so it's a good idea to erect a windbreak around them. It's... it's a trick of the trade."

"Wow, I didn't know that." Amber looked at her with respect. "I'm so glad you're helping me, Poppy. It's great to have someone who knows what they're doing."

"Um... er... thanks," mumbled Poppy, squirming. She had never felt so awful in her life. *Oh God, why did I lie? Why didn't I tell Amber the truth?*

"Hey, listen...I'm going to make a cup of coffee." Amber gave her a warm smile. "Come and join me?"

Poppy glanced towards the house. "Is John up as well?

"Oh, he was up hours ago. He couldn't sleep, so he decided to go down to London early."

"To London?"

"Yes, tomorrow is one of his consulting days and he normally makes sure that he's in London by the night before, so he can go over the patient notes. He won't be back until the weekend, so it's just us girls..." Amber giggled. "Come on, Poppy. You're early anyway, so you've got time."

Poppy already felt bad for lying to Amber, and taking advantage of the girl's hospitality seemed to make things even worse. On the other hand, she was a bit stuck on the work front—she didn't know what to do with the "sick" plants and she'd lost her confidence with regards to planting more things. If she whiled away some time having coffee with Amber, at least it would be less obvious that she was doing nothing in the garden.

"Thanks—that sounds lovely," she said and followed the other girl into the house.

Inside the huge designer kitchen, Poppy watched as her hostess started flipping switches on the gleaming espresso machine which dominated one corner of the counter. The sight of it reminded her of the days when she was stuck in her old London job, getting coffee each morning for her horrible bully of a boss, and in spite of her troubles, she felt a wave of relief and gladness.

"What is it? You've got this strange smile on your face," said Amber, giving her a quizzical look.

"Oh..." Poppy laughed, slightly embarrassed. "I was just thinking how glad I am to be here—living at Hollyhock Cottage and starting a new life. I mean, there are still troubles and stresses... but overall, it's wonderful compared to what I left behind."

Amber handed her a steaming mug of coffee and sat down opposite Poppy with her own mug. "Yes, I know what you mean. My parents were really poor, you know, and when I was growing up, there was always the constant worry of how they were going to put food on the table. I never had new clothes—I always wore hand-me-downs from charity collections—and the shoes I had were always too small and pinched my feet, but we couldn't afford to buy new ones every year…" She smiled at Poppy's incredulous look. "Yes, it's true. And I always swore to myself that when I grew up, I would be rich and live in a big fancy house, surrounded by beautiful things, and with wardrobes full of designer clothes!"

She gestured to the luxurious surroundings around them and gave a tinkle of laughter. "As you say, this is wonderful compared to what I left behind." She put a protective hand on her belly. "And I'm going to make sure that my child has all the things that I never had. He or she is never going to go to bed hungry or be embarrassed to go to school because their clothes look like they've shrunk in the wash or wonder why Santa could never get them anything they wanted for Christmas…"

She leaned back, let out a gusty sigh, and smiled. "It's one of the reasons I said 'Yes' when John asked me to marry him, you know. I knew that he came from a really posh family, and as a doctor, he was going to be rich himself. I knew that as his wife, I'd never want for anything. Oh, don't get me wrong—I do love John... although I don't know if I'd love him quite so much if he wasn't quite so rich!" she added with another giggle.

Poppy made a show of drinking her coffee as she tried to think of what to say. She was slightly shocked at such a blunt confession. She knew, of course, that there were women who married for money, but she had never met anyone who was so open about their mercenary motives. Amber must have read her mind because she gave Poppy a shrewd look and said:

"Are you shocked?"

"Oh... no!" said Poppy, trying to put on a sophisticated air. "I mean, it used to be the normal thing for women to do, didn't it? Like in Jane Austen's time—most women didn't marry for love. They married to 'secure a comfortable home'. And it looks like you managed to do that really well... so good for you!"

Amber gavc a dry smile. "Don't think it's all moonlight and roses. I may look like I have the perfect life, but I pay for it in other ways. Like putting up with John's affairs, for example."

"A-affairs?" Poppy choked on her coffee.

Amber waved a hand. "Oh, John doesn't think I notice, but of course I know. He can't keep it in his trousers, the stupid sod. He was even having an affair with Christine Inglewood, did you know that?"

"Uh... n-no," Poppy stammered, staring at the

other girl as her carefully cultivated theory about John's motive for murder crumbled around her.

"Yes, the whole time the house was being renovated—he was coming up here to meet her. Don't tell me he would be that interested in blinds and bathroom fittings!" Amber gave a cynical laugh. "A couple of times, I could smell her perfume on him when he came home, and once I even overheard him making a phone call to her. He'd sneaked out during one of our house parties in London and I happened to go upstairs to look for a safety pin because one of the guests had split her dress. Anyway, I looked out of our bedroom window and saw him skulking in the bushes below. The window was open and his voice carried up quite clearly. He was talking to Christine, saying some cheesy line about her being the cure for his addiction."

Poppy blinked. "And you didn't mind?" she asked before she could stop herself. Then she flushed and said quickly, "Sorry. It's none of my business—"

"I suppose I minded a bit," said Amber, tilting her head to one side, like someone considering a philosophical question. "But the thing is, I know that at the end of the day, I'm the one that John always comes back to—I'm the one bearing his name and I'm the one with his ring on my finger." She extended her left hand and fluttered her fingers, making the huge solitaire diamond on her fourth finger sparkle brilliantly.

It was an echo of what Nick had said last night and Poppy was taken aback to hear Amber embrace the same sentiments now. She felt suddenly very naïve. She had judged everything by her own ideals and values, without ever pausing to think that there might be other women who felt differently.

"Do you ever confront John about his other women?" she asked.

Amber laughed. "No, why should I? It's fun to watch him trying to skulk around, telling those pathetic lies. And it means that he always feels so racked by guilt that he says yes to anything I ask for. It's how I got him to agree to let me redo the garden here, you know," she added with an impish smile. "It was back around Easter and he'd just broken up with Christine—"

"They've broken up? How do you know?"

She shrugged. "You get to know the signs. John always tires of them after a while and comes crawling back to me. The affair with Christine had been going on for about six months now, so it was about time... Plus they started acting really oddly too. They'd always been a bit hostile towards each other—I think it was an act to put me off the scent—but they started being *really* weird. All stiff and awkward. And John started making excuses to leave the room whenever Christine was around. I just knew." She gave a complacent little smile. "So I saw my chance. John can be a bit bossy—he always wants to decide everything—you know, like where we go on holiday and how many children we're going to have and what I should wear to bed... and he'd originally insisted on formal landscaping for the whole property—all clipped hedges and manicured lawns—with hired help to do all the maintenance work. Well, I told him I wanted a cottage garden and said I wanted to have the whole garden redone." She giggled. "He didn't put up any fuss."

Poppy looked at the girl in front of her with slight awe. She had felt sorry for Amber, being dictated to at every turn by a male-chauvinist husband and being kept like a "little wife"... but she was beginning to realise that Amber Smitheringale was nobody's fool. Nor anybody's victim. In fact, far from being the vapid blonde bimbo, Amber seemed to be the master manipulator in this relationship.

She cleared her throat. "So... um... John definitely isn't seeing Christine anymore?"

"Well, I haven't asked him directly," said Amber with a chuckle. "But yes, I'm pretty sure. I almost feel a bit sorry for Christine, you know. She's always telling me that I need to get a career and she's so clever and successful—she must think that she can always get any man to do what she wants. Anyway, the last time she was here, she mentioned that she's looking into online dating, so I'm sure she'll find someone else soon enough." She tilted her head and looked at Poppy with sudden interest. "What about you? Have you got a chap?"

"Oh... er... no," said Poppy, alarmed to find the conversation turning in her direction. "I mean, I've had a couple of boyfriends in the past but nothing serious."

"So... still foot-loose and fancy-free?"

Poppy laughed. "That's such an old-fashioned phrase. But yes, my heart is still very much my own. In fact, I don't think I've ever been in love. *Really* in love."

"Ah... that just means you haven't met the right man yet," said Amber with a knowing smile. Then she got a gleam in her eye. "What d'you think of Nick?"

"N-Nick?"

"Yes, you know... John's friend—Nick Forrest, the crime writer... tall, dark, and brooding... looks like he stepped straight out of a Gothic romance novel!" Amber giggled.

"Um... well, he's just my neighbour. I never think about him much. I don't know him that well—or really want to," Poppy added hastily.

Amber raised her eyebrows. "You don't like him?"

"Er... we... we just don't seem to get on."

"Well... you know what they say about the thin line between love and hate—"

"That's such a cliché," said Poppy, rolling her eyes. "Anyway, I don't *hate* him. I just... Nick has this way of always saying things that annoy me and make me lose my temper... plus he always wants to be right in everything and... and... I always get this feeling that he's secretly laughing at me—"

"For someone who never thinks about Nick much, you certainly have a lot of reasons," said Amber with a suggestive smile.

Poppy flushed. "No, you're getting the wrong idea... It's just that we've been thrust together a few times recently—"

She caught herself when she heard what she'd said, and a memory of last night, when she and Nick had been *thrust together*—literally, in the cramped coat cupboard —flashed in her mind. She felt her cheeks burn even more. Seeing Amber watching her with amusement, she added hastily:

"Besides, you never know when Nick's going to be as nice as pie or bite your head off—which is really off-putting."

"Yes, I've noticed he's a bit moody" agreed Amber. "But that's just the artistic temperament, isn't it? Goes with the territory. All writers are probably like that."

"Well, I don't need that in my life," said Poppy firmly. "Anyway, I'm too busy now to be thinking about relationships. I've got to focus on the cottage garden and getting my new business up and running."

"Well, you know what they say about all work and no play..." said Amber with another suggestive smile.

"Speaking of work, I... um... I suppose I'd better get back to the garden," said Poppy, keen to end this conversation about her personal life. She smiled and rose from her seat. "Thanks very much for the coffee."

"This was great! We must do it more often," said Amber enthusiastically as she walked Poppy to the French doors. "All the other women in the village seem to be nosy old biddies—there's no one else my age to have a girlie chat with. Plus the only thing people seem to want to talk about these days is Valerie's murder." She rolled her eyes. "You'd think that no one had ever been murdered before!"

"Well, it *is* different when it's on your doorstep—literally, in your case," said Poppy.

"Oh, I know! And believe me, I *have* been racking my brains to see if I could remember anything or anyone odd hanging about Valerie's house that morning, just like the detective sergeant asked me to, but I don't think there's anything—"

"What about the night before?" asked Poppy suddenly, pausing as she was about to step outside.

Amber frowned. "The night before? No, nothing odd..."

"Well, even if it's not 'odd' specifically—just anything you noticed at all. Like a car parked in the lane or if anyone came to see Valerie—"

She snapped her fingers. "Wait a minute... you know what? I've just remembered—I *did* see someone at Valerie's door the night before she was murdered. It was quite late—nearly eleven, I think. Actually, I only saw him because I went out to fetch my sunglasses, which I'd left in the car. I heard voices and looked across, and I saw Valerie at her door, talking to a man."

"What did he look like?" asked Poppy eagerly, thinking suddenly of the intruder at Valerie's house the night before. "Did he have very tanned, leathery skin? And grey hair?"

"Hmm... he did have grey hair—he looked like he was in his sixties, perhaps, but I don't know about leathery skin. He didn't look like someone who worked outdoors—he was very smartly dressed, in fact. In beige chinos and one of those old-fashioned navy blazers... you know the kind I mean? Like, double-breasted, with the brass buttons."

"Did he go into Valerie's house?" Poppy asked.

Amber shook her head. "No, they just talked on the doorstep. He did give her something, though: a bottle."

"A bottle? You mean, like a bottle of wine?"

"It was a similar shape, but it looked more like one of those bottles for homemade cordials and things. You know, with one of those swinging clip tops." Amber gestured with her hands.

"A homemade gift?"

"Yes, I suppose so..."

"Do you think he was a village resident?" Poppy asked.

Amber gave a regretful shake of her head. "I didn't recognise him... but then, I don't know the people in the village that well yet, so I really can't say."

"Was there a car in the lane?"

Amber shook her head.

"Well, it was too late then for the buses to be running, so he must have walked—which means that he's likely to have been a local." Poppy reasoned. "Did you tell the police this?"

"No. He looked very respectable—not like a tattooed biker or a tramp or anything, so I didn't think of him when the sergeant asked me about noticing anything odd."

"You should tell Suza—I mean, Inspector Whittaker as soon as possible. It might be important," urged Poppy.

"All right, I'll ring her as soon as I've showered and dressed." Amber gave a little squeal of excitement. "Do you think this man could be the murderer?"

Well, until twenty minutes ago, I was convinced your husband was the murderer, thought Poppy. Aloud, she said, "Yes, I think he could be the person who poisoned Valerie Winkle."

CHAPTER NINETEEN

When Poppy finally stepped outside again, she was startled to see a man in the garden. He was around the side of the house, pushing a lawnmower across the strip of grass that ran along the side of the Smitheringales' property. He had his back to her and all she could see was grey hair pulled back in a low ponytail and a wiry frame clad in old-fashioned green overalls. She guessed that this was the handyman that John and Amber—and also Suzanne—had mentioned, who did odd jobs for the Smitheringales. *What was his name? Joe something... Joe Fabbri. Yes, that was it.*

She was about to ignore him and continue on to her flower bed when he turned with the mower and his face came into view. Poppy felt her heart give a kick of recognition. It was the same tanned, leathery face that she had glimpsed through the crack in the coat cupboard at Valerie's place last night!

He noticed her staring and switched off the lawnmower. Poppy expected him to say something, but he simply regarded her mutely. The silence stretched until she couldn't bear it anymore and she approached him at last with a hesitant smile, saying:

"Hi… I'm Poppy. I've been hired to help Amber plant the flower beds. And you must be Joe?"

His face looked old—somewhere in his late sixties, perhaps—but the knotted muscles of his hands and forearms seemed to belong to a younger man. And when he grasped Poppy's outstretched hand, he gave it such a firm squeeze that she nearly yelped.

"Yeah."

The silence stretched again. Poppy cleared her throat.

"Um… I hear that you help the Smitheringales around the house?"

"Yeah."

"So… um… do you live in the village?"

"Yeah."

"Oh… because… I thought maybe if I need help fixing things—I live in Hollyhock Cottage—maybe I could call you as well?"

"Yeah."

Poppy gave up. The plant pots provided more

conversation than this man! She had hoped to somehow mention Valerie's house and see if she could get a reaction out of him, but his laconic manner made it impossible to lead the conversation in any direction. Sighing, she gave him a polite nod and was about to turn away when he spoke up:

"You hiding something?"

Poppy jerked back, her heart beating unsteadily. He was nodding at the canvas screen around the dying plants.

"Oh... er... um... that's just... it's a temporary thing..." she stammered. "Nothing to worry about... it's just a protective screen around the plants and... er—" Her voice rose to a panicked yelp as he left his lawnmower and started walking towards the flower bed. "NO! WAIT! THERE'S NOTHING TO SEE!"

She rushed after him, trying to prevent him from getting closer, but short of physically grabbing his arm and holding him back, she couldn't really stop him. So all she could do was watch in trepidation as he stopped beside the screen and peered over the top of the canvas.

"It's... I... er... um..." Poppy racked her brains for something to say, something that could excuse the scene of devastation in front of them.

"Transplant shock."

Poppy stopped and stared at him. "I... I'm sorry?" She followed his gaze to the plants, then it dawned on her that he was offering her an answer. "Oh... you mean, that's what's wrong with them?

"Reckon."

Poppy took that to mean "yes". She saw him looking at her and, for a moment, she was tempted to brush him off, to try and salvage her pride and gloss over everything again with an *"Oh, don't worry—I've got everything under control"* kind of comment...

But it was silly pride that had got her into this predicament in the first place. She swallowed, then said in a small voice: "I'm just a beginner and I think I've messed up really badly. Is... is there any way to save them?"

"Mebbe."

She was beginning to realise that Joe was a man of few words. Still, his interest seemed genuine and she was grateful to have any kind of help she could get.

"Can you please tell me what I need to do?" she asked humbly.

He ran a practised eye over the plants, then glanced up at the sky, where the sun was blazing mercilessly. "Hot day. Keep 'em shaded. Chance to recover. You watered 'em?"

Poppy nodded vigorously. "Oh yes—I really flooded them last night, and watered them again this morning." She looked doubtfully at the brown, shrivelled leaves on the roses. "Will the leaves turn back to green?"

"Naw."

"So... so they'll remain looking like that?" said

Poppy in dismay.

He glanced at the roses. "Give 'em a trim. Grow new leaves. No problem."

Poppy began to feel a glimmer of hope. "And do I need to give them anything else? Like fertiliser?"

"Naw!" His voice was sharp. "No fertiliser until recovered. Burn 'em, otherwise. Need new leaves, new roots—spread out and down into soil. Suck up water better."

"Oh... and when I planted them, I damaged the roots. That's why they're struggling, especially as it's been so hot!" said Poppy, beginning to understand. She gave him a grateful look. "Thank you... thank you so much. I'm going to do everything you said and keep my fingers crossed!"

Joe's eyes crinkled at the corners as his lips twitched upwards slightly. Then he gave her a thoughtful look, his eyes lingering on her face, and said: "Look a bit like Mary."

"Mary...? Oh, you mean my grandmother, Mary Lancaster."

He inclined his head. "Yeah. Knew her as a girl." His gaze swept her face again. "Same eyes."

"Did you know my mother?" asked Poppy eagerly. "Holly Lancaster?"

"Only as a mite."

"Only as a—? Oh, you mean only when she was a little girl?"

He inclined his head again. "Ran away from home."

"Yes, when she was sixteen. I... I think she tried to get back in touch when she got pregnant with me but... I don't think she was very welcome."

Poppy tried to keep the bitter reproach out of her voice, but she wasn't quite successful. She saw Joe glance at her face again and had an uncomfortable feeling that those old eyes saw more than she wanted to show.

"Proud woman, Mary," he said at last. "Never could admit she was wrong."

Something in the way he said that made Poppy wonder if there was a personal story behind that comment. And she realised suddenly that she might be more like her grandmother than she realised—not just in her looks but also in clinging to her stubborn pride and struggling to admit that she was wrong.

"Dad left you?" Joe asked suddenly.

For a moment, Poppy was taken aback. So far, most people in the village had been quite coy when trying to worm information out of her. Oh, it was obvious that they were gagging to know about her father, but it was usually done with sly questions and suggestive glances. But now, to her surprise, she found that she actually preferred Joe's blunt approach and answered more readily than usual:

"No, I never knew him. My... my mother was a groupie—she followed some rock bands around in the States," she explained as he looked at her blankly. "But she left them and came back to

England when she got pregnant with me."

"Your dad's a Yank?"

Poppy shrugged. "Probably. I don't know. My mother only told me that he was a musician in one of the bands, but I don't know anything more than that."

"You try to find him?"

"I... yes... I mean, no... I used to think that he would come and find *me*..." Poppy shook her head and gave a wistful smile. "I thought... I thought that he would appear on my doorstep one day and take me back to this amazing new life in Hollywood..." She sighed. "But it was just a stupid dream."

"Reckon it's good to dream sometimes."

Poppy looked up in surprise, then smiled gratefully. "Yes, but I've got a new dream now. A better one. I decided that I'm going to make that amazing new life myself! I'm not going to sit around, waiting for my father to show up and rescue me."

He looked at her silently for a moment, then gave a slow, approving nod. Poppy flushed, feeling suddenly that she had said too much, revealed too much of herself. Hurriedly, she changed the subject.

"Um... Isn't it horrible what happened to Valerie? Did you do any work for her?"

"Yeah."

"Oh yes, that's right... I remember Suzanne—I mean, Inspector Whittaker—telling me that you dropped off some tools at her place the morning she died?"

His eyes took on a wary expression. "Looked fine."

"And um... have you been back to her house since the murder?" Poppy asked casually.

Joe's eyes went cold and his expression became stony. "Naw." Turning away, he muttered: "Got to get on. Another job."

And he restarted the lawnmower and roared away without another look at her.

CHAPTER TWENTY

Poppy spent the rest of the morning following Joe's advice. Using some more stakes and canvas garden bags, she erected a temporary shade over the wilting plants so that they were protected from the hot sun. Then she watered them carefully again and piled up some mulch around their bases, to keep the roots as cool as possible. Finally, she went around with a pair of hand pruners and trimmed off the worst of the dried leaves and shrivelled stems. At last, she stood back to survey the flower bed. She sighed; she had done all she could. It was a waiting game now. All she could do was cross her fingers and hope...

She packed up her things and left the Smitheringales' place, thinking how lucky it was that Amber seemed to have gone out for the day. At least it meant that she didn't have to explain the increasingly strange arrangement of wooden stakes and canvas fabric draped around the flower bed. Still, the other girl was bound to see it when she got home and would be wondering what on earth was going on.

I'll have to face her and tell her the truth tomorrow, Poppy thought, wincing at the prospect. But she couldn't go on lying and covering up—she had to own up to her mistakes and confess the truth. Maybe Amber would invite her in for coffee again tomorrow morning and she could break the news then. The companionable setting would make things easier—it would feel more like two friends having a chat and sharing their secrets...

Speaking of secrets... Poppy's mind drifted back to the chat she'd had with Amber that morning. She had been surprised by how much the other girl had opened up, how much Amber had revealed about her personal life... In fact, Poppy had been so preoccupied with the dying plants that she hadn't really given much thought to the conversation... until now.

She thought over Amber's revelations again and wondered what this could mean for the murder investigation. Could she have been wrong about John being the murderer, after all? If there was no threat from Amber finding out about the affair, then there was really no motive for him to kill Valerie. Of course, *John* didn't know that Amber knew, so he could still have been worried and wanted to silence his nosy neighbour. But somehow, after seeing Amber's matter-of-fact reaction to her husband's infidelity, Poppy was beginning to think that Nick was right and John wouldn't consider an affair to be a great threat to his marriage—certainly not enough to risk something like murder.

But if it wasn't John, then who could it have been? Prunella Shaw? The police certainly weren't ruling her out. Anger and revenge were powerful motives. And—based on the story that Mrs Peabody had recounted about Prunella attacking the fellow delphinium exhibitor—the woman *did* have a history of violence when she lost her temper.

Except that this wasn't an impulsive, violent crime, Poppy reminded herself. Poison was about as premeditated as you could get. Somebody went to all the trouble of getting hold of some aconitine... and then figured out a way to get Valerie to eat or drink it...

So who else could it be? The man that Amber had seen the night before the murder? Had he brought something for Valerie—a homemade wine, perhaps—that had been doctored with aconitine? Was it possible that Valerie had been poisoned the night before rather than the morning she'd died, like previously thought? But Suzanne had been adamant that Valerie couldn't have had such a lethal amount of poison in her system for long without showing symptoms.

Then there was Joe the handyman... where did he fit in all this? He'd admitted to going to Valerie's place that morning to deliver some tools, but was that all? Despite only getting a quick glimpse, Poppy was sure Joe had been the man creeping around the murdered woman's house last night. What had he been searching for?

And what about the letters that she and Nick had found? Valerie *had* been blackmailing someone, all right. It might not have been John, but it could easily have been someone else in the village, especially given what Prunella had said about *"people with secrets in this village... secrets that they're willing to commit murder for..."*

Poppy was so deep in thought that she wasn't looking where she was going and nearly crashed into another person coming down the narrow village lane, in the opposite direction. A person who was muttering absent-mindedly to himself and also not looking where he was going.

"Bertie!" Poppy exclaimed. She was surprised to find him on this side of the village. As far as she knew, the eccentric inventor rarely left his property.

He tottered sideways for a moment, struggling to balance the pile of things he was holding in his arms. Einstein barked in delight as he saw Poppy and launched himself forwards to say hello, straining at the end of the leash that was looped around one of Bertie's wrists.

"Oops!" Poppy cried as the old man was yanked

sideways by the terrier and nearly toppled over. “Here! Let me help you—” She reached out and relieved Bertie of half his load.

“Ah… thank you, my dear.” He smiled gratefully at her. “I did wonder if it might be a bit much to carry, but it seemed fine when I set out.”

“Where are you going with all this stuff?” asked Poppy, looking down at the odd assortment of things, from textbooks to jam doughnuts, electric wires to a cage containing a white laboratory rat with beady red eyes.

“I’m going to Desmond Fothergill’s house,” said Bertie. “The Oxfordshire Entrepreneurs Association is having another meeting there and I wanted to show them my ultra-sonic rat repeller again—now that I’ve refined the prototype.” He grinned and indicated the doughnuts. “And I’ve made some jam doughnuts too. It’s my special recipe, which includes a regenerative follicular hormone to stimulate hair growth. I thought the gentlemen of the Association would appreciate some as I noticed several of them are going quite bald.”

“Er… I probably wouldn’t mention that, Bertie,” said Poppy, thinking of the elaborate comb-overs she had seen amongst the members that night.

He looked surprised. “Why? It’s true.”

“Yes, but they probably don’t like anyone pointing it out. Besides, you can’t just put hormones in people’s doughnuts without telling them,” she chided.

"But it works so well," he said, patting his own head. "My hair just won't stop growing now!"

Poppy eyed the wild grey mop on his head, which looked like several birds might be happily nesting in there, and thought that going bald might be the lesser of two evils.

"I think you should at least tell them what's in the doughnuts, so they can decide for themselves," she said gently. "It isn't fair otherwise."

"Humph. I suppose you're right," he said, looking like a small boy who had been denied his favourite toy. Then he made a tetchy sound and turned to the terrier, who was whining excitedly and jumping up to try and reach the rat in the cage. "Now, stop that, Einstein! I told you: you can't chase Fahrenheit."

Poppy hesitated, then said: "Listen, Bertie, why don't I come with you and help you carry your things?"

It wasn't a completely innocent offer. She had remembered Amber's description of the man she'd seen visiting Valerie late at night—*"very smartly dressed, in fact. In beige chinos and one of those old-fashioned navy blazers... you know the kind I mean? Like, double-breasted, with the brass buttons"*—and thought that it could easily match any member of the Oxfordshire Entrepreneurs Association. Going with Bertie would be a great excuse to mingle with the members and see if any of them might have known the murdered woman.

"Ah, thank you, my dear...It's just around the

corner."

They arrived at the house a few minutes later and Bertie rang the doorbell. They waited. There was a long pause. Bertie pushed the bell again.

"Um... are you sure they're expecting you?" asked Poppy.

"Certainly. Desmond Fothergill—who is the president of the Association—told me that they'd be happy to view my invention again at the next meeting."

Poppy glanced at the empty street around them and said, "Strange... you'd think there would be more cars parked around here, if the members were all here for the meeting..."

Bertie pressed the doorbell again, keeping his thumb on the button for several seconds, and after a moment, they heard faint footsteps somewhere in the house. They seemed to be coming from above, accompanied by the sound of muffled thumping on wood, and Poppy realised that someone was probably coming down the stairs from the second storey.

Then the door was flung open and Desmond Fothergill stood in the doorway. He looked very different from the last time Poppy had seen him—he was dressed in a man's silk dressing gown, the old-fashioned kind with a paisley pattern, wide lapels, and contrasting silk piping that Noël Coward would have been proud of. It was hastily belted around his waist and so long that it almost touched the floor.

Poppy wondered why on earth he was wearing a dressing gown at three o'clock in the afternoon. *Perhaps he was ill and they had got the poor man out of bed?* His cheeks seemed to be quite flushed and his lips very red, and she wondered if he was slightly feverish.

"Dr Noble!" he said, looking taken aback.

"Hello, Mr Fothergill! I'm here for the meeting," said Bertie, beaming at him.

"The... the meeting?" He gaped at them.

"Yes, the Oxfordshire Entrepreneurs Association meeting? You said I could show my ultrasonic rat repeller again," Bertie reminded him.

"But the meeting isn't until next week," said Fothergill.

"Oh dear... have I got the date wrong?" said Bertie, scratching his head. "I was so sure it was today." He peered into the house. "So the other members are not here?"

"No. I'm alone." Fothergill shifted slightly and the dressing gown parted at the bottom, revealing his bare legs, thrust, incongruously, into black patent leather shoes. Poppy blinked. Was it her imagination or did his legs have an odd sheen to them? Like the satin shimmer you see on stockings...

He caught her looking at his legs and jerked the folds of his dressing gown closed. "I... er... I was having a nap," he said in a dignified manner. "I had... um... a bad headache."

"Ah! A headache—I have just the thing to help you!" cried Bertie, reaching excitedly into his inner jacket pocket and pulling out a circular tangle of metal spikes and wires that looked like a cross between a crown of thorns and a TV antenna.

Poppy groaned. She had seen that contraption of Bertie's before. In fact, she'd even had the misfortune of wearing it on her head once, and she still winced when she remembered the mayhem it had caused.

"What on earth is that?" Fothergill stared.

"It's my Neural Cranio-Analeptic Equaliser," said Bertie proudly. "I created it to help heal the brain after a head injury, but it would work on headaches too. On a lower setting, of course, otherwise the electromagnetic pulses might fry the hair on your head. Almost had that happen, actually, the last time I tried it—but don't worry, I've adjusted the conductivity... Here, you hold this for a moment." Bertie shoved the rat cage into Fothergill's startled arms, then quickly unfolded the contraption, stretched it into shape, and placed it on the other man's head. "Now, we just need to find a plug..."

He marched into the house, with Einstein trotting at his heels.

"Wait—Dr Noble!"

Fothergill hurried after him, still carrying the rat, and Poppy followed. They found the old inventor in the sitting room, looking around for a free socket.

"Er—Dr Noble... thank you for the offer... very

kind, I'm sure... but I'm quite all right now. My headache's all gone," said Fothergill, hastily pulling the tangle of spikes and wires off his head.

Bertie looked crestfallen at not being able to use his invention. "Are you sure? It would still be beneficial even if there is no longer any pain; it would help to synchronise the neural pathways—"

"No, no, I'm fine, I assure you," said Fothergill, shifting nervously as Einstein began trotting around him, eyeing the rat cage he was holding with interest.

Suddenly, the terrier jumped up and lunged for the cage. The rat squealed and thrashed in a panic, causing Fothergill to cry out in surprise and drop it. The cage door burst open; the rat shot out and disappeared behind the sofa. Einstein pounced after it but missed, grabbing the end of Fothergill's dressing gown belt instead.

"Hey! Let go!" gasped Fothergill, trying to pull the belt out of the dog's mouth.

Einstein wagged his tail in delight, obviously thinking that this was a new game. He clamped his teeth down even harder and began tugging on the belt in earnest, growling excitedly the whole time.

"Bad boy, Einstein! Let go of the man's belt," admonished Bertie.

"Drop it, Einstein!" Poppy ordered.

"Let go of me! *Let go of me!*" Fothergill shouted.

The more everyone yelled at him, the harder the terrier tugged at the belt, twisting his head from side to side and throwing his little body back with all his might.

"No... *NO... LET GO!*" cried Fothergill almost hysterically, one hand clamped around his middle, the other trying to wrestle the belt from the dog.

He gave a desperate jerk which finally wrenched the belt from Einstein's mouth, but the force sent him sprawling backwards. He crashed into the sofa and tumbled to the ground.

"Oh! Mr Fothergill, are you all righ—" Poppy broke off and stared.

Desmond Fothergill staggered to his feet. His dressing gown had come completely undone and the front had parted to reveal his hairy chest and beer belly... dressed in a black silk lace teddy. Underneath it, he was wearing suspenders attached to lace stockings that covered his hairy legs with a nylon shimmer.

There was a long, horrible silence.

Then Bertie said brightly: "Ah, my wife used to have a black lace teddy like that. She said it was wonderfully comfortable to sleep in. Do you sleep in yours too?"

Oh my God... groaned Poppy inwardly.

"Uh... I... er... *ahem...* mmm... uh... er..." Desmond Fothergill struggled for words.

Poppy carefully avoided looking at him. She didn't know who was more embarrassed, her or the red-faced man standing opposite. Fothergill hastily yanked the dressing gown tight around him, belting it firmly once more. Then he cleared his throat and said in a deep, manly voice:

"*Ahem-ahem*... Well, that was unfortunate... I do hope you have another rat to use for your demonstration, Dr Noble, as I doubt we'll find that one again... Er... Perhaps it would be good to keep your dog at home in the future..."

Poppy stared at him incredulously. Was he really expecting them to pretend that they hadn't seen anything and carry on as normal?

"Uh... right... now, I must bid you good day... very busy... you'll have to excuse me..." Fothergill babbled as he bundled them unceremoniously towards the front door.

Then Poppy spotted something in the entrance hall and stopped short.

"Mr Fothergill—are those homemade?" She pointed to the collection of glass bottles in a crate next to the door. Each bottle had a clip top and was filled with a slightly cloudy, pale green liquid.

"Yes, yes, elderflower cordial... I make some every year and share it with the other villagers," he mumbled. "Here, would you like one?"

He thrust a bottle at her and then, before she could say another word, pushed her and Bertie out of the front door and shut it in their faces.

CHAPTER TWENTY-ONE

Poppy walked slowly next to Bertie as they headed back across the village. He seemed to be lost in a world of his own, muttering equations to himself, and she was glad that she didn't have to make conversation. If her thoughts had been muddled earlier, now her head was really spinning.

So Desmond Fothergill likes to dress up as a woman... she mused. He must have been indulging in his private hobby upstairs when they arrived and their insistent ringing at the door had forced him to come down with only the dressing gown as a hasty covering. Those flushed cheeks and red lips that she had thought were signs of fever were probably the remnants of rouge and lipstick that he had hastily scrubbed off.

No wonder he had been so touchy a few nights

ago when Bertie had mentioned him being in touch with his "feminine side". And if his reaction was anything to go by, Fothergill would be mortified if anyone found out about his little secret. His standing in the community, his reputation as a respected businessman, as president of the Oxfordshire Entrepreneurs Association, as a model of conventional British manhood... everything would be destroyed if the other villagers found out about his fetish.

The question was, how far would he be willing to go to keep things a secret? As far as *murder*?

If nothing else, he was certainly a prime candidate for extortion. Poppy thought of the "black teddy" mentioned in the blackmail letters that Valerie had written. She had assumed that it referred to a teddy bear, but now she realised that it could just as easily have been referring to a piece of women's lingerie.

She looked down at the bottle of elderflower cordial in her hands. Was it a coincidence that Desmond Fothergill made homemade elderflower cordial—and that Amber had seen a respectable-looking, middle-aged gentleman giving Valerie a cordial bottle the night before she was murdered...?

"Would you like to come in for some tea, my dear?"

Poppy looked up and realised with surprise that they were standing in the lane midway between Hollyhock Cottage and Bertie's house. She had been so immersed in her thoughts, she hadn't even realised that they'd arrived back.

"Why don't we have tea at my place, Bertie?" she suggested, thinking that it would be more comfortable than his ramshackle kitchen, with laboratory equipment all over the place. Besides, she was never quite certain of what she was eating or drinking while at the old inventor's place (and in particular, whether it was explosive or not).

"Oh, that would be lovely!" The old man followed her enthusiastically into the cottage garden and up the path to the front door, with Einstein scampering eagerly ahead.

"I must say, my dear, you have done a marvellous job in the garden here!" he added, looking around admiringly.

"Oh! Thank you." Poppy flushed with pleasure at his compliment.

She paused on the path and looked around them. Everything seemed golden, the soft afternoon light surrounding the plants and flowers like liquid amber, backlighting the leaves and petals. A bee buzzed lazily as it flew past, its legs heavy with pollen, and somewhere by the wall, in the shade of the trees, a chiffchaff warbled loudly. Poppy had been so busy with the landscaping job over at the Smitheringales' the last few days, she hadn't had much time to spend at Hollyhock Cottage, and now she was surprised to realise how much she'd missed it.

She was also surprised to see how much had changed. She used to think that you just planted a garden—plonked plants in the ground, positioned them according to your design, staked them, watered them—and that was that. But she was beginning to realise how wrong she had been. A garden wasn't like furniture or décor placed in a room, rigid and immobile. A garden was *alive*: it grew, breathed, stretched, faded, bloomed, died, slept, regenerated... constantly... all the time...

Yes, even in the few days that she had been absent, things had changed and there was so much new to see: that rosemary bush over there—it had grown several new shoots... and the foxgloves and delphiniums were so tall now that they were all leaning precariously... and the honeysuckle—surely it hadn't been that high up the wall the last time she'd looked at it? Then there were the roses: some which had been rampant with flowers were now bare of blooms, with nothing more than a few ragged petals clinging to the hips—and others which had only been showing a few buds were now bursting into flower...

Poppy felt like she was rediscovering the garden all over again and it was an intoxicating feeling. It was also a balm to her soul to see all the plants looking so green and healthy. Her disastrous experience at the Smitheringales' had really knocked her confidence and made her wonder again if she was crazy to think that she could resurrect her grandmother's garden nursery. But now, looking at this beautiful garden, she felt her spirits restored.

Inside the house, she settled Bertie at the wooden table in the kitchen, then went to the pantry to hunt for some biscuits to go with the tea. As she stepped in, however, she was dismayed to find a mess waiting for her. It looked like several boxes and bags of items had suddenly split open and spilled their contents everywhere. There were biscuit crumbs, cereal grains, and dried pasta shells littered all over the shelves and pantry floor.

What on earth had happened here? As she bent closer to look, Poppy saw that there was actually a little hole gnawed at the base of the cereal box and the same tooth marks on several of the spilled pasta shells. She also noticed several small black droppings on the shelves.

"*Uuugghh!*" she cried, recoiling in disgust.

"What is it, my dear?" asked Bertie, coming to join her in the pantry.

"I found a nest of rats in the shed at the back of the garden the other day... and now it looks like they're in the house!" Poppy gestured to the shelf with the spilled pasta. "They've been helping themselves to things in the pantry. Ugh!"

Bertie adjusted his spectacles and peered at the mess. "Hmm... yes... *Rattus norvegicus*—the common brown rat—highly intelligent, very adept at making the most of any food source available, perfectly adapted to living alongside man—"

"What am I going to do?" asked Poppy. "I can't have rats in here. They could carry disease and it's so unhygienic. But oh, I can't bear the thought of putting down rat poison. It causes such a horrible death. Besides—" she glanced at the terrier at her feet, "—I'd be worried that Einstein or Oren might eat some of the bait by mistake."

"Ah, not to worry, my dear—what you need is my ultrasonic rat repeller!"

Poppy gave him a sideways look. "Er… not the thing that you were showing the Oxford Entrepreneurs Association, which exploded the other night?"

Bertie waved a dismissive hand. "That was a prototype. As I was going to tell the members of the Association at today's meeting—er, if it *had* been today—I have vastly improved it. I have removed the explosive element and it works now simply by ultrasonic waves, enhanced by radio waves."

"Um… thanks, Bertie, but I don't think—"

"It's extremely effective!" insisted Bertie. "I have tested it very successfully in my own house—I haven't seen a sniff of a rat since." He put a hand down to pat the terrier's head. "Poor Einstein is a bit miffed, actually. He's a terrific ratter, you know, and when we first moved in, he'd spend hours every day hunting for rats. Used to bring them all back to me. Very off-putting, I must say, to wake up in the morning and find a pile of dead rats by the bed. But since I have activated the repeller, I'm afraid poor Einstein has been deprived of his fun."

Poppy thought of Bertie's absent-mindedness and his tendency to leave half-drunk mugs of tea and half-eaten plates of food everywhere, and was impressed that his home could be rodent-free. Perhaps his invention *was* worth trying after all...

"And you're in luck, my dear!" added Bertie excitedly. "I've actually made a second, smaller version of the initial prototype. In fact, I had been planning to show it to the Association today. If you hang on a tick, I've got it here somewhere... just need to find it..." He rummaged in the ancient leather briefcase that he always carried. "Ah! Here it is!"

He pulled something out of the case and handed it to Poppy. She looked down.

"This is it?" she said, not quite able to keep the disappointment out of her voice. She didn't know what she had been expecting but it wasn't this unassuming little black gadget, barely bigger than a match box.

"It may not look like much, but you'll be amazed by what it does!" Bertie said. "Most ultrasonic pest repellers are not very effective, you see—rodents, in particular, quickly become desensitised to the sounds, and the sound waves themselves are short range and very weak. But *my* version addresses all these problems! It transmits in an unpredictable pattern and it also uses a transformer to convert some of the ultrasonic waves into radio waves, which can travel better through obstacles. Now... you switch it on here, see?"

Bertie turned the gadget over to show her a flip switch next to a small dial on the underside of the box. "The switch turns it on and off, and the dial determines the direction. Make sure it's turned clockwise, my dear—otherwise, if you have it the other way, it will reverse the sound waves and actually attract rats."

Poppy gave him a doubtful look but took the device and pocketed it. "All right. Thanks, Bertie. I'll try it and let you know." She looked back at the pantry with a sigh. "I'll clean up the mess later and then find a good spot to place the repeller. In the meantime, do you mind having your tea without any biscuits?"

"We could have some of my jam doughnuts?" suggested Bertie.

"No," said Poppy firmly. "I don't need any more hair growing on my body, thank you very much." She led him back to the table and filled the kettle, then set it to boil. Then she leaned against the kitchen counter and said: "By the way, Bertie, when we were at Desmond Fothergill's house just now and saw his... er... black teddy, you mentioned that your wife—"

His face softened. "Ah, yes... Audrey had one just like that."

Poppy looked at him curiously. "Um... I never

realised that you were married."

His shoulders slumped, and he looked suddenly much older. "Yes, many years ago."

"Is she...?"

"She's dead." His face crumpled. "And it's all my fault."

Poppy stared, completely at a loss over what to say. Einstein whined softly and nuzzled his master's hand, and Bertie gave a little sigh as he looked away into the distance. There was a long silence.

At last, Poppy cleared her throat and said: "I... I'm sorry, Bertie."

She was dying to ask him what he meant—why was his wife's death his fault? Was it connected in some way to the mysterious death of the research student and to his losing his professorship at the university? There were so many mysteries surrounding Dr Bertram Noble, and she wished that she had some answers. But as she glanced at Bertie's face again, she couldn't bring herself to ask more. In fact, she was beginning to feel bad for even broaching the subject. Bertie was always so cheerful, so full of boundless enthusiasm and childlike excitement, that it was disturbing to see him so subdued and sad.

The boiling of the kettle broke the silence and Poppy jumped up to make the tea, glad to have something to busy herself with. As she set the two mugs on the table, she said, in a bid to distract Bertie:

"You were right about the poison used to kill Valerie Winkle, you know. It *was* a plant alkaloid—it was something called aconitine."

"Ah, aconitine!" said Bertie, brightening. "From *Aconitum napellus*—also known as monkshood or wolfsbane, because it was once used to kill wolves. In fact, in folklore, it is even believed to have the power to repel werewolves."

"And it's apparently found in many gardens?" asked Poppy, remembering what Suzanne had said.

Bertie nodded. "And growing wild too, across the British Isles. It belongs to the *Ranunculaceae* family of flowering plants, which also includes common favourites like buttercups, clematis, and delphiniums."

Poppy's ears pricked up. *Delphiniums again.* "They're related to delphiniums?"

"Yes, you could say that they are sort of cousins."

"So... someone who knows a lot about delphiniums would know a lot about *Aconitum* too?"

"Certainly. Their flowers even look quite similar. Delphiniums are toxic too, of course, but not as lethal as *Aconitum*, which is known as the 'queen of poisons'. And for good reason! Gardeners who have just touched *Aconitum* buds with their bare hands have felt their fingers go numb. The poison can cross the skin barrier, you see—it's a lipophilic molecule. Nicotine is another plant alkaloid which can be absorbed by contact."

"Oh, is that why smokers end up with yellow stains on their fingers?"

"Ah, well, the tar in cigarettes also contributes to that. Of course, the stain will fade with time once you stop smoking, as the dead layer of epidermis sloughs off and new skin replaces it."

Poppy thought back to the bottle of cordial that Desmond Fothergill had given her. "Bertie—you said that alkaloids are really bitter. Could you disguise their taste, for example in a drink?"

"Yes, I suppose so. If you add enough sugar, you can usually mask most unpleasant flavours."

"And how long does it take for the poison to start showing symptoms? I mean, if you were poisoned late at night, could the symptoms not start showing until the next morning?"

Bertie frowned. "Well, aconitine is normally very fast acting, but depending on the other contents of the stomach... and of course, if you are sleeping, then everything slows down—all metabolic processes and bodily functions... It would still be unusual though. You're much more likely to start showing symptoms within a few minutes to a few hours."

"So maybe she didn't drink some cordial until the next morning..." Poppy mused.

"Eh? I beg your pardon?" Bertie looked at her quizzically.

Poppy laughed. She was becoming as bad as the old inventor! "Nothing, Bertie—I was just thinking out loud."

"Ah! That's a very beneficial practice, my dear!" said Bertie enthusiastically. "Research studies have shown that talking to yourself out loud can have cognitive benefits and improve your performance on difficult tasks. It can even improve memory and learning. I talk to myself all the time," he said proudly.

Poppy looked at Bertie with affection and smiled. Perhaps there was a method to his madness after all!

CHAPTER TWENTY-TWO

After Bertie and Einstein had left, Poppy set about the unpleasant task of cleaning up the mess in the pantry. She had barely started, however, when the doorbell rang. Glancing at the clock—which showed that it was nearly eight o'clock—she wondered who could be calling at this time, and was surprised when she went to the door to find an elegant, dark-haired woman standing on the doorstep. It was Detective Inspector Suzanne Whittaker.

"Hello!" said Poppy, smiling. "This is a nice surprise."

"I know it's a bit late—I hope I'm not disturbing you or anything?"

"No, not at all. Come in! Would you like a cuppa?"

A few minutes later, Poppy found herself once again at the kitchen table, nursing a mug of tea and talking about Valerie Winkle's murder. Or rather, listening to Suzanne talk about it. It seemed that the police investigation wasn't making much progress and Suzanne's voice was filled with frustration as she went over the case. Poppy listened and commiserated and offered suggestions where she could. She was flattered but also slightly surprised and puzzled that the other woman was confiding so much in her. Something must have shown in her expression because, at length, Suzanne trailed off and said, with a shamefaced laugh:

"You must be wondering why on earth I'm here, telling you all this stuff."

"No, no, I'm honoured that you feel you can trust me—"

"Funnily enough, I do trust you," said Suzanne, looking at Poppy thoughtfully. "It goes against all reason—and official police rules, I might add—to be sharing information with a civilian, but... I don't know... call it instinct or women's intuition, if you like—" She broke off and gave a cynical laugh. "In fact, that's the whole point. If I admitted to something like 'women's intuition' down at the station, I'd probably be lynched!"

"Really?" Poppy raised her eyebrows.

Suzanne sighed. "Joining the Force has been tougher than I expected. I feel like I'm always working overtime to prove that I'm 'as good as the boys', and not show any uncertainty or weakness. The men never do, you know. In fact, sometimes I almost get the impression that some of them are watching me, hoping to see me mess up..."

"Oh, I'm sure that's not true," Poppy protested.

"You might be surprised," said Suzanne dryly. "It hasn't helped that I've risen up through the ranks to a senior position pretty quickly. I think some of them don't like a woman standing out, in what has always been a male-dominated profession. And there are no other senior female officers around locally, so it gets a bit lonely sometimes." She gave Poppy an embarrassed smile. "You're a very good listener... I suppose I was looking for a friend without even realising it."

Poppy was incredibly touched. Suzanne always seemed so capable and confident, so certain of what she wanted from life and how to get it; Poppy had always envied her elegant beauty and cool self-assurance. It was a pleasant surprise to discover that the other woman admired her as well.

"Oh... I... I'd love to be your friend," she stammered. Then she heard how she sounded and giggled. "We sound like two schoolgirls in the playground."

Suzanne burst out laughing and the seriousness of the moment dissolved. When they had calmed down again, she grinned at Poppy and said:

"I've also got a selfish motive for discussing the

case with you. I like the way your mind works. You're very sharp and you see things from different angles. It reminds me of Nick, actually."

"Nick?" said Poppy in surprise.

Suzanne nodded. "I often used to come and see Nick, to discuss cases I'm working on… just to get his perspective. He was someone—someone outside the station—I could trust, and relax with." She made a rueful face. "Well, except that invariably, we'd end up disagreeing about something. He'd make some ridiculous suggestion—like breaking into a suspect's house to search their place without a warrant—and I'd feel obliged to rebuke him for breaking the law… and then he'd accuse me of having no imagination and I'd accuse him of having no morals… and we'd always end up having a huge fight."

"Er… right," said Poppy, shifting uncomfortably and thinking of last night when she and Nick had done exactly that: broken into a suspect's house to search it without a warrant!

Suzanne sighed. "It was one of the reasons we broke up, you know. Nick's very impetuous and incredibly impatient, and he really believes that the ends justifies the means. As a practising police officer, I'd always feel it was my duty to reprimand him. I always laugh, you know, when I see those fantasies about sexy policewomen… Take it from me, having to be the nagging voice of the law all the time really puts a damper on any romantic relationship."

She leaned back suddenly and gave Poppy a rueful look. "Sorry. That was probably too much information. Don't know why I started going on about Nick—"

"No, it's all right... I can imagine that it must have been really frustrating."

"Especially when he turns out to be right!" said Suzanne, rolling her eyes. She sighed again. "It makes me doubt myself and wonder if I should be willing to be a bit more unorthodox sometimes. Would I be a better detective if I ignored the law occasionally? Like with this case: Nick rang me this morning and told me that I should consider searching Valerie's cottage again. It wasn't an idle proposal, either—it was a very specific suggestion, telling me to go over the place myself 'just in case the junior chaps missed something'—those were his words." She furrowed her brow. "Now why would Nick say that?"

Because he knows that your junior detective constables did *miss something*, thought Poppy. She licked her lips and said with a forced laugh:

"Maybe he's got 'man's intuition' or something. I mean, he's a crime writer, isn't he? So he spends a lot of time thinking up motives for murder... you know, like... um... blackmail! That's a popular reason, isn't it? People often commit murder when they're being blackmailed and they're feeling desperate..."

Suzanne raised her eyebrows. “Are you suggesting that Valerie was blackmailing someone?” Her eyes narrowed. “Do you and Nick know something I don’t?”

Poppy swallowed. “No! I mean—I don’t know what Nick knows—but I just...” She groped around for a reason. “Um... it was something Prunella said, actually,” she said at last. “She told me that there were people in the village with secrets that they would do anything to hide—maybe even commit murder for.” She hesitated, then took a deep breath and added, “And... and I think that person could be Desmond Fothergill.”

“Desmond Fothergill?” Suzanne looked surprised.

Poppy felt bad exposing the man’s furtive hobby, but it could be relevant to the investigation. Besides, she’d been very touched by Suzanne’s trust in her—she felt that she ought to return that trust in some way.

“I happened to visit his house unexpectedly earlier today and caught him unawares. He... um... was wearing women’s lingerie.”

Suzanne gave a low whistle, sounding more like her fellow “macho cops” than she realised. “So Fothergill is a cross-dresser?”

“Yes... not that I think that’s a big deal in itself.” Poppy shrugged. “I mean, what a man chooses to do in the privacy of his own home is his business, as long as he’s not hurting anyone. But I doubt

Fothergill is so philosophical about it, and I don't think many of the more conservative villagers would be either. In fact, based on his reaction, I think he would do anything to keep his secret hidden."

"That may be true, but it doesn't mean that he was being blackmailed by Valerie," Suzanne pointed out.

"No, but his black teddy was mentioned in the—" Poppy broke off, realising suddenly that she couldn't tell Suzanne about the "black teddy" reference in the blackmail letters without revealing that she had broken into Valerie's house last night. She cleared her throat and hastily amended her statement to: "Um... I mean, I also noticed that Fothergill had a crate of homemade elderflower cordial by his front door. He said that he makes it every year, to give away to the other villagers. And Amber Smitheringale told me that she noticed a man calling on Valerie the night before she died. He didn't go in, but he gave Valerie something—a bottle with a clip top, like a cordial bottle."

"What? Amber didn't mention that in her statement!" exclaimed Suzanne.

"She didn't think of it at the time," Poppy explained. "She said that your sergeant asked her whether she'd noticed 'anything odd' and she didn't think that it really counted as 'odd'. The man looked very respectable, you see. He was very smartly dressed, in a blazer and chinos, and she thought 'odd' meant something like a tramp or tattooed gangster or something."

"And yet... *you* managed to get her to remember this potentially important lead."

"Oh. Well. We were just chatting and I suppose I happened to jog her memory. I asked her if she remembered anything—even if it didn't seem 'odd' specifically."

"Hmm..." Suzanne gave her an appraising look. "I'm beginning to think our junior constables need to come and take lessons from you on how to interview witnesses."

Poppy blushed. "I didn't do anything special. Really. And Amber's description of the man she saw *could* match Desmond Fothergill. What if it *was* him and he had called on Valerie to give her a bottle of his homemade elderflower cordial... which was spiked with aconitine?"

Suzanne shook her head. "That's one thing that I *have* had clarification on, actually. I'm still waiting for the full post-mortem report—there's been a terrible backlog and all cases have been delayed—but the preliminary findings show that Valerie didn't actually have the poison in her stomach."

Poppy stared at the other woman. "Not in her stomach? But then how—? I thought you said they'd definitely found aconitine in her system?"

"In her system, yes, but not in her stomach. Which means that she didn't eat or drink the poison."

"Then how did she—?"

Suzanne shrugged. “That’s one of the mysteries we haven’t solved yet. I suppose someone could have injected it into her, using a hypodermic needle and a syringe... So far, the forensic pathologist hasn’t found any sign of needle marks, but that doesn’t necessarily mean anything. There are places to inject where it’s not easy to be seen. All the drug addicts know that.”

The words “hypodermic needle” and “syringe” made Poppy think of doctors and her thoughts flashed back to John Smitheringale once more. Could she have been right about him after all?

Suzanne was still talking: “...it’s a shame, in a way, that Valerie wasn’t a smoker, as they bruise more easily and take longer to heal, so a needle mark might have been more noticeable—”

“Oh!” Poppy cried, sitting up straight. “Smokers! Nicotine!”

Suzanne looked at her in puzzlement. “I’m sorry?”

Poppy said excitedly, “I think I know how Valerie was poisoned!”

CHAPTER TWENTY-THREE

"It was you mentioning smoking—it made me think of something Bertie said!" Poppy explained. "That's my neighbour, Dr Bertram Noble."

"Yes, I know Dr Noble—"

"He guessed that the poison was a plant alkaloid, even before your toxicology reports confirmed it, and then earlier this evening, when we were talking about the murder, he mentioned that aconitine—like nicotine—can be absorbed across the skin. Apparently, even touching the flower buds with your bare hands can make your fingers feel numb. I just thought of it now..."

Suzanne frowned. "So you think Valerie touched the poison with her hands?"

Poppy nodded excitedly. "Yes! In fact, it might have worked even faster absorbed through the skin since it could have entered the blood stream directly, rather than having to go through the stomach." She leaned forwards eagerly. "Did the forensic pathologist say anything about Valerie's hands? Have they tested them to see if there are any traces of poison?"

"I don't know. I imagine they will do it as part of the full post-mortem but... Hang on a sec—let me ring Forensics now."

Poppy glanced at the clock on the wall and raised her eyebrows. "Would they still be working now?"

Suzanne gave a short laugh as she dialled a number. "*I'd* still be working at the station now if I hadn't decided to come and talk to you. We're all working crazy hours at the moment, to try and get on top of the case load. Shame there's no overtime in the CID..." She broke off as her phone was answered and turned away to speak.

Poppy got up and left the table to give Suzanne some privacy. She made some fresh tea and, when she returned to the table, she found Suzanne looking at something on her phone screen.

"You were right," Suzanne said, her voice vibrating with excitement. "There was blistering on Valerie's palms and when they tested it, they found traces of aconitine on her skin. And they also found some traces on the handle of the hand fork that she had been using when she collapsed."

She turned her phone around and pointed to the

photo displayed on the screen. It showed several items in a clear plastic evidence bag, one of which was a small hand fork with a wooden handle.

"These were the things found next to Valerie's body—they must have fallen out of her gardening apron: a spool of garden twine, some plant labels, a pruning knife, the hand fork, and a pair of gloves. She'd obviously taken the gloves off for some reason." Suzanne shook her head. "Her bad luck. If she had been wearing them, she might still be alive."

Poppy glanced at the photo, barely listening. Her mind was on something else: Joe the handyman had delivered some gardening tools to Valerie the morning she had died. *Gardening tools.* How easy it would have been for him to have coated one of the handles with the poison before giving them to Valerie... Then she thought of last night and the handyman's strange late-night visit to Valerie's house. Had he been looking for the hand fork that had been tampered with, so that no one would find traces of poison on the handle?

"Poppy?"

Poppy jumped and came back to herself, to find Suzanne looking at her quizzically.

"Sorry... I was just... um... my mind wandered a bit."

She wanted to tell Suzanne her suspicions about Joe, but two things held her back. One was that—once again—she couldn't report his presence in

Valerie's house without admitting to Suzanne that she herself had been trespassing there, and had even entered a crime scene without permission. Yes, it had been Nick's idea, but she had gone along with it. Somehow she didn't think Suzanne would be understanding and she hated the thought of destroying the woman's newfound trust in her and respect for her.

The second reason was quite simply that she liked Joe Fabbri. It was a lame reason, she knew, but somehow she just couldn't believe the old handyman could murder anyone. In spite of his abrupt, laconic manner, there had been something wise and good about him. But... was she just biased because he had been kind and helped her with the dying plants at the Smitheringales'?

Suzanne's voice brought her out of her thoughts:

"...anyway, this is a fantastic breakthrough," the detective inspector was saying enthusiastically. "We just need to focus on who could have had access to Valerie's gardening tools and the knowledge and opportunity to doctor them with aconitine. They must have used a paste made up of the roots, and maybe some kind of abrasive as well—like fine sand—which would break the skin and make it easier for the poison to penetrate."

Poppy hesitated, knowing that there was still a chance to say something about Joe Fabbri. Then she pushed the thought away and said instead:

"Have you had dinner yet? Would you like to stay

and have something with me? It'll only be something simple, but—"

"I'd love to but I grabbed a sandwich earlier," said Suzanne with a regretful smile. "Plus I've got to be back at the station early tomorrow morning, so I'd better get to bed. Maybe some other time?"

"Oh yes, pop round whenever you like." Poppy looked at Suzanne shyly. "I really enjoyed our chat."

"Me too. And thank you! You've helped to unearth a strong lead." She laughed. "I knew it was a good idea to come and talk to you."

A few minutes later, Poppy stood at the front door and watched as Suzanne walked slowly down the path and disappeared through the gate. Poppy paused for a moment before shutting the front door, gazing around the garden again and enjoying the peaceful ambience. It was nearly nine now and twilight was falling, drawing the long summer day to a close.

Through the trees to her left, she caught a glimpse of lights from Nick's property. They were the garden lights—the house itself was dark—and she wondered if Nick was out for the evening. She also wondered where a certain ginger tomcat was. She had been surprised, when she'd arrived back home, not to find Oren waiting for her (although in hindsight, since she had been accompanied by Bertie and Oren's arch-enemy, Einstein, it was probably just as well), and now she wondered if the big orange cat was all right.

Has he had dinner? What if he's hungry and Nick didn't feed him before going out? Then she laughed at her own anxious thoughts and reminded herself that Oren wasn't her cat. He had managed fine for all that time before she had arrived to live in Hollyhock Cottage and there was no doubt that he knew how to take care of himself. And Nick—for all his grumbling about the cat—obviously loved his feline housemate and took good care of him. Oren's glossy orange fur and sleek, muscular body were more than enough proof of that.

She turned back into the house and was about to shut the door when her heart gave a little skip at the sound of a familiar demanding voice:

"*N-ow... N-ow...?*"

She whirled around to see Oren strolling up the path. She had no idea where he had come from—she had been looking in that direction only a minute ago and had seen no sign of him. It was as if he had materialised straight out of the undergrowth.

"Hello, you..." She smiled in delight as she crouched down and reached out to pat him.

He came up to her and stood purring, with his eyes narrowed in pleasure, as she scratched his chin. Then he followed her into the house and accepted his usual bowl of cat food, as was his due. When he had finished, she expected him to head for his favourite armchair and begin his evening ablutions, but to her surprise, Oren seemed suddenly to have a "post-dinner high". He began zooming around the room, chasing and pouncing on pretend prey, jumping up on things and getting into all sorts of places that he shouldn't.

"Hey, Oren... no, get off the kitchen counter! No, no... don't climb in the bin either—oh *Oren!* You bloody cat—now you've tipped the rubbish all over the floor... Stop that... *Stop that!* Grrr... if you keep this up, I'm going to chuck you out!"

"*N-ow?*" said Oren cheekily, eyeing her from the seat of one of the chairs at the table.

"Yes, now!" Poppy gave him a mock glare. "You're just being a little monster! Go and sleep in your armchair, and let me make my dinner."

"*No-oow*!" said Oren.

He jumped down off the chair and trotted over to investigate the huge canvas bag that Poppy used to lug her things to the Smitheringales' and back daily. She'd dumped the bag in a corner of the kitchen, like she usually did when she got back home, and now the ginger tom sniffed it curiously. He pawed at the bag, causing it to tip over onto its side and spill some of its contents onto the floor.

"Oren...!" Poppy groaned.

She had been lazy earlier that day and hadn't rinsed her tools before stuffing them back into the bag. Now a trowel, hand fork, and cultivator tumbled out, still covered in dirt, and soil scattered everywhere, all over the kitchen floor. Poppy hissed in annoyance and knelt down next to the bag to clear up the mess. But Oren hadn't finished. He was now trying to climb into the bag, burrowing into its depths and pushing more items out with his back legs, so that they spread the dirt even farther.

"Oren! Stop it!" cried Poppy in exasperation.

She reached for the cat and dragged him out of the bag, earning herself a petulant "*No-o-o-ow!*" and a sulky look from Oren as he struggled to be free. She set him down on the floor and he stalked off, lashing his tail in a temper. Poppy turned her attention back to the bag and sighed as she eyed all the items scattered around her. How had she ended up with so much junk in the bag? She must have been shoving things inside without paying much attention, every time she tidied up at the Smitheringales' each day.

She began to sort through the items, thinking that perhaps this was a good opportunity to get rid of some things, or at least remove them and store them in a different place. That jar of slow-release fertiliser, for example—it could just be left at the Smitheringales' place until the end of the job. There was no need for her to lug it back and forth every day... And those empty plastic containers could be chucked—she wasn't going to use them again... and why on earth did she have so many pairs of gloves in here? She only really needed one working pair. The trowels too—there seemed to be a duplicate pair—she must have taken two different ones from her grandmother's greenhouse, intending to try both to see which felt more comfortable, and then forgot to return the other one... and what was this?

Poppy frowned as she lifted a cotton pouch out of the pile. It was covered in a pretty floral pattern and, as she pulled the flap open, she saw that there was yet another set of hand tools inside. *Oh for heaven's sake!* she thought, annoyed with herself. How many duplicate sets of garden tools had she been lugging around? No wonder her canvas bag felt heavier and heavier every day! Besides, these weren't even hers—this was the set that Amber had shown her on the first day, which Christine Inglewood had given to her as a gift—

Poppy froze, staring down at the set of hand tools in the pouch. They had beautiful wooden handles, highly polished, with an ornamental pattern engraved around the tip.

The pattern looked familiar...

Then it came to her, like a smack in the face. It was the same pattern she had seen in a photo recently—on the handle of the hand fork that had been found with Valerie Winkle's body.

CHAPTER TWENTY-FOUR

Poppy felt her heart beating with painful jerks as a sickening realisation began to dawn on her. In her mind's eye, she saw that fateful day once again: Valerie standing on the other side of the hedge, lecturing her on how to plant the roses... and then stepping through the gap and coming over to bossily show her how to do it. The murdered woman had knelt down by the hole and vigorously loosened the soil using a hand fork with a wooden handle...

Poppy had assumed that it was Valerie's own tool, which she had brought with her when she stepped through the hedge. Now, however, as she strained her memory, she remembered seeing—out of the corner of her eye—Valerie bending and picking something up from the pile of tools next to the flower bed. Poppy hadn't paid much attention to it at the time; she'd been keeping her head down and just hoping that the annoying woman would go away. But now she realised that Valerie must have scooped up a hand fork from the pile as she'd walked past.

Suzanne Whittaker had said that it was Valerie's bad luck that she hadn't been wearing gloves when she decided to be a busybody that day. Well, it had been even more bad luck when Valerie had inadvertently picked up *that* hand fork—the one from the pouch. It must have been lying at the top of the tool pile, with the flap open and the tools half out when Valerie had walked past.

So… if the tool that Valerie had been holding was the one which was coated with poison… and that tool was a gift from Christine… then there was only one conclusion: Christine Inglewood was the murderer.

Poppy rocked back on her heels. She couldn't believe it. *Christine?* And that also meant that Valerie Winkle wasn't the intended victim at all! Yes, it was obvious now that the poison had been intended for *Amber*. That was who Christine had given the gift to. John Smitheringale's mistress had wanted to kill his wife… and had ended up killing his neighbour by mistake instead.

It also explained something else… Poppy recalled the morning when they had all sat having tea together and Christine had been so upset when Amber had announced that she wasn't allowed to do any more gardening until the end of her pregnancy. Poppy had thought that the woman was simply showing feminist indignation at Amber being dictated to by her husband—but in fact, she had been dismayed that her carefully prepared murder weapon might miss its target.

It also explained the expression of pity that had flashed across Christine's face when Amber introduced them and announced that Poppy was going to help her in the garden. Christine had obviously realised that *Poppy* might be the one to touch the poisoned hand fork instead.

Poppy shook her head. She couldn't believe that she had actually *liked* the woman and thought her to be kind. When Christine had come to visit Hollyhock Cottage yesterday, it hadn't been because of a desire to make over the cottage—no, it had been because Christine had wanted to pump her for information about the murder investigation, to see if the police had any strong suspects.

Well, the police are going to have a new suspect now, thought Poppy grimly, getting up and going to find her phone. She dialled Suzanne's number and waited impatiently as the phone rang... and rang... and rang...

Why wasn't Suzanne answering? Poppy frowned. She glanced at the clock again, then remembered that the detective inspector had mentioned that she was heading straight for bed. It was only about half an hour since Suzanne had left—would she have gone to sleep already? Or perhaps she was having a bath—something to help her relax and unwind after her long day...

Then Poppy thought suddenly of Amber, and for some reason she felt a flicker of unease. Deciding to try Suzanne again in a few minutes, she called Amber instead and listened once more to a phone ringing repetitively. She tried the Smitheringales' land line and, again, no one answered. The feeling of unease grew and before she knew what she was doing, she was dialling John Smitheringale.

"Poppy!" He sounded surprised. "Er—how are you?"

"I'm fine. Um... I was trying to get hold of Amber, actually. She's not answering her mobile. I just wondered if you might know where she is?"

John sounded puzzled. "She should be at the house in Bunnington. I came down to London this morning—I've got consultations all day tomorrow—but she didn't come with me. Have you tried the landline?"

"Yes. No one is answering that either."

"That's odd. I know she didn't have any big plans today. She told me she might pop to the shops and then Christine was coming over and they were going over the plans for decorating the nursery—"

"*What?* When? When was Christine coming?" asked Poppy urgently.

"I don't know—sometime this evening, I think... Hello? Hello?"

Poppy whirled and ran for the door. She raced down the garden path, out the gate and up the lane, then ran through the winding streets of Bunnington as fast as she could. It was dark and the narrow streets weren't very well lit but she was familiar with the route, having gone back and forth daily in the past week, and she didn't slacken her pace.

She arrived at last in the lane in which Valerie's house and the Smitheringales' property were situated. Like most country lanes, it didn't have street lights and relied on the lights from the houses to illuminate the area. Valerie's cottage was pitch dark, but the Smitheringales' larger house was fairly well lit—there were solar garden lamps lining the path alongside the clipped hedges, and a large light above the front door. Everything looked quiet and normal.

Then Poppy noticed the car parked in the lane, right in front of the house. She caught her breath: it was Christine's sleek grey BMW.

The driver's seat was empty but there was someone in the front passenger seat. The lights from the house outlined the figure dimly. Poppy caught the glint of blonde hair.

Amber.

She rushed over to the car.

"Amber? Amber?" she called, frantically rapping her knuckles against the passenger window.

The figure didn't move. Amber was facing away from the window, so that all Poppy could see was the back of her blonde head. The other girl looked as if she was slumped against the seat. Poppy felt her heart give an uncomfortable lurch.

She tried the passenger door. It was locked. She ran around the car to the driver's side and yanked at the door. To her relief, it swung open and she dived in, half crawling onto the driver's seat to reach Amber. The blonde girl had her eyes shut. For a moment, Poppy thought that she was simply asleep, but when she reached out and gently shook Amber's shoulder, the girl didn't respond.

"Amber? Amber?"

She shook harder. Nothing. The girl's head lolled against the headrest. Poppy felt her nerves tighten. This was no natural sleep. She leaned closer, straining her ears for the sound of breathing, and felt relief wash over her as she saw the faint rise and fall of Amber's chest. The girl was breathing, but very shallowly.

What's happened to her? Poppy wondered. She had to get her to a hospital immediately. She leaned in farther, trying to figure out how to get the girl out of the car—then she heard a noise behind her.

Poppy jerked around, but not fast enough.

There was a blur of motion and a dazzling beam of light shone straight into her eyes, blinding her. Then someone grabbed her from behind. She gasped as her head was yanked back and something thrust into her parted lips. Liquid sprayed into her mouth. She gasped again, and coughed and choked, but the cruel grip on her neck didn't loosen, and the bitter-tasting liquid was pumped into her mouth again.

"N-no!" Poppy cried, trying to free her arms.

But her limbs felt strangely leaden. She tried to summon the energy to move them but then... she wasn't sure she wanted to anymore. She felt a dreamy state steal over her... it was almost as if she were floating...

Dimly, she felt her body slump down against the car seat and a tiny part of her brain protested, struggled, fought... but it was like a very distant voice at the bottom of a very deep well that was growing fainter every moment...

Her eyes fluttered shut... and darkness came...

CHAPTER TWENTY-FIVE

Poppy came slowly back to consciousness, like someone rising from the deep—except that there was something down there that didn't want to let her go. Like a sea monster that had wrapped its tentacles around her legs, it yanked her back every time she broke the surface, pulling her under again, so that she drifted down once more into that twilight state between dreaming and waking...

Then suddenly she was thrust out of the depths again, and this time her fingers met rock... She clawed her way out and clung on as the waves broke over her, then receded...

Poppy blinked and looked groggily around. She felt sick and dizzy, and every breath seemed to take a massive effort. Her fingers flexed against a cold, hard surface but it was cement, not rock, and she was not stranded on some boulder rising out of the sea but was slumped instead against a brick wall. She couldn't see very well at first but she could sense that she was in a large space. Indoors, not out, with a roof very high above her.

She stirred and tried to sit up, but her body felt almost as if it wasn't connected to her head. Her arms lay limp and useless by her side, her legs splayed out, and all she could feel was a strange tingling, like "pins and needles" running unpleasantly up and down her skin.

She turned her head with an effort and looked around. It was dark, with only a weak, flickering light coming from the bare fluorescent tube that hummed noisily in the shadows above her head. There was also a pale light seeping in through small windows set high in the walls—enough so that she was able to see.

She was in a huge, cavernous area, cold and damp, with the smell of dust in the stale air. Crumbling plaster and cracked cement littered the floors, amidst small piles of broken glass and drifts of dried brown leaves. A stack of wooden pallets stood in the corner, and rusty pipes ran around the room and across the ceiling.

An old warehouse... or a factory? Whatever it was, it was obviously shut down and abandoned—at least by humans. Her ears caught a faint squeaking and she stiffened. She knew that sound. *Rats.* She shifted restlessly, and her arm brushed against something—cold, clammy skin. She jerked around so quickly that she nearly lost her balance, then she saw that it was Amber. The other girl was also propped against the wall next to her.

"Amber?" Poppy whispered.

The other girl didn't stir, but in the dim light, Poppy could just make out the faint movement of Amber's chest. She felt some of her tension ease. Slowly, she tried once more to rise, leaning on the wall for support. She had managed to raise herself to a sort of half crouch when she heard the sound of footsteps echoing on the hard cement floor, and a moment later, Christine strode in from a set of double doors at the other end of the building.

Poppy felt a surge of panic and scrabbled frantically, trying to get to her feet, but her uncoordinated limbs betrayed her and she collapsed in a heap against the base of the wall.

Christine came slowly across to stand above the two girls, looking down at them with a contemptuous smile.

"Ah… you've woken up sooner than I expected."

Poppy swallowed past the nausea in her throat and croaked, "What have you done to us?"

Christine waved an airy hand. "Oh, don't worry—nothing dire. Just a spritz of fentanyl to give you a nice little sleep." She smiled. "Lucky for me that one of my clients was a recent cancer patient; it was the work of a moment to slip his fentanyl spray out of his medicine cabinet and into my handbag. Of course, I wasn't quite sure of the dosage—apparently this is pretty powerful stuff and an overdose can easily kill you—but..." She shrugged and laughed. "Who cares? You and Amber are both going to die anyway. It would have probably made things easier for me if you had overdosed... and nicer for you when your body goes in the incinerator," she added.

"The... the incinerator?" Poppy gasped.

She followed Christine's gaze and realised that there was an enormous cement burner at the far end of the room, its dark hulk looming ominously out of the shadows. She swallowed and tried to control the panicked thudding of her heart. A sense of unreality swept over her. *This can't be happening to me... Being dumped by a murderer into an incinerator—that's the kind of thing that happens in movies or on TV, not in real life...*

"You... you can't do this..." she said hoarsely. "People will find us... The villagers will notice your car... John knew that you were coming over tonight to see Amber and he'll tell the police and they'll know you did it—"

Christine laughed. "Oh, I think not. I didn't drive through the village—the bottling factory is at the end of the same lane that the houses are on, so I just drove down from the Smitheringales' house until the road ended. No one comes down here, especially at night. And I took care of all the details before I left the house—I made sure it all looked neat and tidy, just as if Amber had planned to go out... In fact, you did me a favour when you arrived like you did: there would have been more questions asked if I had been the only person last seen with Amber, but now I can say that I left the two of you in a cosy tête-à-tête..." She gave a malicious smile. "I might even add a few juicy extra details like, for instance, how distressed you looked when you arrived and how you were rambling incoherently... And of course, once the incinerator is finished with its job, there will be no trace of your bodies. You will simply be two women who disappeared—another tragic missing persons case."

"The police aren't stupid! People don't just disappear for no reason. They'll be suspicious; they'll search the area—"

Christine laughed again. "So they'll be busy scurrying around, won't they? Anyway, it's only in books and movies that everything gets neatly wrapped up, with a reason and explanation for everything. That doesn't happen in real life. Even if the police were to find some trace of your bodies and realise that there was foul play involved... so what? There are murder cases where the police never fully solve the mystery and can only take guesses at what really happened."

"I know Suzanne—Inspector Whittaker. She'd never be satisfied with that," said Poppy desperately.

Christine smirked. "Well, you'll never know, will

you?"

She turned away and strolled over to the incinerator, where she began fiddling with some of the buttons on the control panel. Poppy felt sick despair wash over her. She wanted to get up, to run, but her legs were so shaky, she could barely stand. Besides, even if she were able to hobble across the room and get out through the double doors, she couldn't leave Amber behind. And there was no way she would be strong enough to drag the unconscious girl with her. From the nonchalant way Christine had turned her back and walked off, it was obvious that the interior designer knew how weak her prisoners were and was confident that they would be no trouble.

It was that arrogance which cut through Poppy's haze of despair and lit a spark of anger inside her. Just a tiny flame at first, but one which burned steadily, growing stronger and brighter.

No, I'm not going to just roll over with a whimper and let Christine win, thought Poppy grimly. She was weak and dizzy and there probably wasn't much she could do to resist—but she wasn't going to give in without a fight.

CHAPTER TWENTY-SIX

Poppy began to look around for something that she might be able to use as a weapon. It wasn't very encouraging. The floor was bare around her, save for those little chunks of cement and crumbling plaster. There wasn't even a piece of broken glass large enough to use as a weapon. The wooden pallets in the corner might have yielded something—perhaps she could have broken off a plank of wood to use as a sort of club—but they were too far away. In any case, she doubted that she would have the strength to dismantle anything...

Poppy felt panic take hold once more and had to resist the urge to give in to despair again. Then she remembered that Christine hadn't tied her hands and feet. The woman obviously thought the effects of the fentanyl would incapacitate her prisoners enough. Poppy slid her fingers into her pockets, feeling for anything she could find. She knew she didn't have her phone—she had dropped it in her rush to leave Hollyhock Cottage and get across to Amber's house—but she was hoping there might be something else...

Ah! Her fingers closed around something small and rectangular. Keeping a wary eye on Christine, she pulled it eagerly out of her pocket. Then her face fell as she saw the small black device. *Oh. It's just Bertie's stupid ultrasonic rat repeller.* Great. What was the use of that? Like making all the rats in the factory run away was really going to help her right now—

Wait.

Poppy turned the device over and stared down at the dial on the back. She heard Bertie's voice again, saying:

"...and the dial determines the direction. Make sure it's turned clockwise, my dear—otherwise, if you have it the other way, it will reverse the sound waves and actually attract rats."

It sounded ludicrous—how could reversing the direction of the sound waves *attract* the rats? And yet... and yet... what if it worked? Besides, what other option did she have?

Poppy threw a furtive glance across the room at Christine's unsuspecting back, then she looked back down and slowly turned the dial anticlockwise, as far as it would go. She had barely done that when the sound of footsteps approaching warned her that Christine was returning.

"Now, I've enjoyed our little chat, but I'm afraid it's time—"

"Wait, Christine—" Poppy said, letting a little quaver come into her voice. The more weak and scared she sounded, the less Christine would be on her guard. "Please, don't do this. I know you're not a bad person—I know you don't really want to kill anyone. What happened to Valerie was an accident—"

"That was no accident," Christine spat. "That was all carefully researched and planned. I even prepared a decoy plant!"

"A decoy plant?" Poppy looked at her, genuinely puzzled.

"To divert suspicion away from the hand fork, of course!" said Christine impatiently. "I managed to find a potted monkshood plant and snipped off some of the buds to make a concentrated paste, to smear on the fork handle. Then I was going to find a convenient moment to stick the original monkshood plant in amongst the other plants waiting to be put into the beds. That way, everyone would just think that Amber had bought one to plant in her garden and there was a tragic accident. It's the kind of thing that could easily happen with an inexperienced gardener."

She paused and scowled. "Although you're

right—the part with Valerie getting the poison *was* an accident. That stupid cow! Always being a busybody and sticking her oar in everywhere. Well, she paid for it this time, didn't she? If she had minded her own business, she might still be alive—and *Amber* would have been poisoned, like I planned."

"*Why?*" Poppy asked. "Why would you want to kill Amber? What's she ever done to you?"

Christine looked at her, her eyes frighteningly calm and blank. "Oh, nothing in particular. She's just in the way, that's all."

"In the way?"

"Yes. John wouldn't leave her, you see. In fact, he even tried to end our affair back at Easter. He told me that we were finished, that he didn't want to see me anymore, that he was going back to her, his darling little wife..." Her voice hardened and the expression on her face became ugly. "Did he really think he could dump me like that? Cast me aside like an old shoe he no longer wanted? *Me?*"

Poppy recoiled slightly, surprised at the sudden change in Christine. Gone was that statue-like stillness, the unnatural calm and the cool, controlled voice. Instead, the woman's eyes were smouldering and two bright spots of colour now burned in her thin face.

Christine jabbed a finger at her own chest. "I'm not going to let him leave me. No, not this time! This time, I'm going to make him keep his promise... I'm going to make him stay with me and Mummy... and take me to school... and hold me when I'm scared... and tuck me into bed at night..."

Poppy stared at the woman in front of her, bewildered by the change again. The sudden aggression was gone, the eyes no longer burning with anger—they were soft and unfocused now, and her lips were pulled back in a dreamy smile. Poppy realised suddenly that Christine wasn't talking about John Smitheringale anymore. No, she was talking about another man—a man who had abandoned Christine and her mother when she was just seven years old... a man she had never been able to forgive or forget...

In spite of the situation, Poppy felt a flicker of sympathy for the other woman. She could understand what it was like to yearn desperately for a father. "Christine..." she cut in gently. "John isn't your dad. Hanging on to him isn't going to make your father come back, nor is killing his wife going to make him love you or want to stay with you—"

"Shut up!" Christine hissed. "What do you know? You haven't even got a man," she sneered. Then she made an impatient gesture with her hands. "I don't know why we're wasting time talking about this anyway. I need to get back to Oxford and sort out my alibi..."

And she came forwards with a purposeful look in her eyes. Poppy braced herself, her fingers tightening around the ultrasonic device that was still clutched in her right hand. She felt for the switch and flicked it to the ON position, then she eyed the approaching woman, trying to judge the distance between them. She would only have one chance...

Luck was with her. As Christine drew near, Amber began to stir. The girl's eyelids fluttered and she moaned softly.

"Aha... so little Miss Perfect is waking up too," said Christine, turning away, momentarily distracted.

Poppy lunged for her. She had hoped to grab Christine with both arms and shove her hard against the wall—but she had underestimated how weak and rubbery her own legs still were. She staggered as she pushed herself to her feet, lurching sideways and crashing into Christine with her arms and legs flailing. The woman cried out angrily as they went down in a heap.

For a split second, they lay tangled together, then Poppy scrambled to get on top. She threw one arm around the other woman's shoulder, trying to pin her down with the weight of her own body whilst, with the other hand, she groped for Christine's pockets. The other woman was wearing tight-fitting designer jeans and, for a horrible second, Poppy thought that all the pockets were false ones, simply stitched on for the look. Then her fingers found the edge of a flap and she pulled it open and shoved the ultrasonic device in.

And not a second too soon. Christine had been cursing and struggling against her and it had taken all of Poppy's meagre strength to hold her down, but now the interior designer twisted her body with a violent movement and shoved Poppy off.

"What do you think you're doing?" Christine snarled.

Poppy fell back, panting, waiting for the device to do something. But nothing happened.

Christine gave a jeering laugh. "Did you think you could mess with me? *Me?*"

She picked up the handbag she had dropped and pulled out a small cylindrical object, with a pump on one end. Poppy's eyes widened as she recognised the fentanyl spray. She started to back away but Christine was faster. Her hand shot out and grabbed the collar of Poppy's T-shirt, twisting the fabric and yanking her close.

"N-no... no! Let go! Let go of me!" Poppy cried, leaning backwards.

"Hold... still..." Christine mumbled, trying to aim the spray bottle at Poppy's face.

Poppy flung her head from side to side, trying to avoid the nozzle, and thrashed around, trying to wrench out of Christine's grasp. But the other woman's grip was merciless. And Poppy found, to her anguish, that her legs kept buckling beneath her. *It's the fentanyl,* she thought wildly. Even though her mind was clearing and the nausea was fading, the drug was still affecting her muscles and her coordination. If it was still this bad after her first dose earlier, a new dose would probably kill her. She couldn't let Christine spray her again!

Poppy felt panic wash over her anew. She had been clinging to the silly hope that Bertie's device would do something, the literal *deux ex machina* that would save her life—but she realised now that she had been stupid. How had she expected a silly invention to save her—

Then she caught her breath as she heard something above the sound of their harsh breathing. She thought she was imagining it at first... but no, there it was again...!

Squeaks. Getting louder and louder.

Poppy's heart skipped a beat. Could it be...?

Something warm and furry\ brushed against her legs, then jumped onto Christine's back and crawled up to her shoulder. Another brown shape appeared out of nowhere and began climbing up Christine's leg, clinging to her jeans.

Christine gasped and let Poppy go, staggering in confusion. Instantly, she was surrounded by a mass of brown furry bodies. Poppy stumbled back, staring.

Rats. Rats everywhere.

"Aaagghh!" Christine screamed, her eyes bulging. "N-nooooo! Get off! *Get off me!*"

She screamed again and flailed her arms, trying to brush them away from her, but the rats paid no heed. They swarmed around her and surged up her body, climbing on each other to reach her. The air was filled with excited squeaking, which almost drowned out Christine's terrified cries.

Poppy whirled and hobbled for the double doors, her mind already trying to think of a way to call for help... then she jerked to a halt as she saw a small red box mounted on the wall, with a glass panel across the front and the words "FIRE – Break Glass" in large letters.

Of course! The fire alarm! That would bring help faster than anything else. Poppy hurried across and smacked her hand on the panel, triggering the alarm. A shrill ringing filled the air, drowning out the squeaking of the rats.

Poppy sagged against the wall and let out the breath that she hadn't realised she had been holding. She glanced across the room: Christine had sagged to the ground as well and now sat in a huddle, with rats still climbing all over her. An uneasy thought struck Poppy: what were the rats doing? She'd wanted Christine stopped, but she didn't want her to be eaten alive or something!

Poppy pushed away from the wall and hurried back to the other woman, but she hadn't gone a few steps when she relaxed. The rats weren't biting or scratching. No, in fact, they all seemed to be trying to snuggle as close to Christine as possible!

Poppy felt a hysterical giggle bubble up in her throat as she stared at the scene in front of her. Oh God—she hated to admit it, but Nick Forrest might have been right again: rats could be cuddly after all.

It was hard to believe that, only a few minutes ago, Christine Inglewood had intended to viciously murder her. All menace had gone out of the interior designer now. She was a gibbering wreck: her face was smudged with dirt, her clothes torn and dishevelled, and her sleek bob of hair now standing up in all directions as two rats busily tried to make a nest amongst the strands. Four other rats were curled up in her lap, a little one was trying to climb into her jacket pocket, and a large brown rat sat on her shoulder, attempting to groom her ear.

And that was how the firemen found her when they rushed into the building ten minutes later. They stopped in confusion at the lack of smoke or fire, then stared open-mouthed at the woman surrounded by rats. Slowly, they turned and looked at the other two girls, their faces bewildered.

Poppy met their questioning looks with a smile and said with a shrug, “She had it coming to her—she was an absolute pest.”

CHAPTER TWENTY-SEVEN

"Oh my lordy Lord, Poppy—look at the state of this place! The rust on those taps… and the stains on the cooker… and that kettle looks like it hasn't been scrubbed in centuries! I can't believe you've been using it like that."

"It didn't look *that* dirty," Poppy protested. "I did give it a rinse—"

"A rinse? *A rinse?* This thing needs more than a rinse! It needs a good scouring out. And I hope you didn't use that excuse for a scrubbing sponge—it looks like an entire bacterial colony is living in there," said Nell, shaking her head in disgust.

She bent to rummage in the shopping bags she'd brought, then straightened up again with a fresh packet of scouring pads in her hands. Rolling up her sleeves, she approached the kitchen sink with a combative gleam in her eyes.

Poppy smiled to herself. Nell had only arrived at Hollyhock Cottage two hours ago, but already they were settling into their familiar routines—just like old times, when they had been living together in London. After Nell had heard about what happened at the bottling factory, she had insisted on coming up to Oxfordshire immediately, despite Poppy's protests; and when she turned up on the doorstep, complete with suitcase, an armful of cleaning supplies, and a flask of homemade chicken soup, Poppy had been secretly glad.

Not that she would have admitted it to anyone, but she had felt a bit fragile since coming home from the hospital. The effects of the fentanyl had worn off fairly quickly but the memories of the frightening experience had lingered. So it had been very nice to suddenly find herself not having to be alone—to sip the hot nourishing soup, tell Nell about the whole ordeal, and be generally fussed over.

Now she leaned back in the chair and watched with amusement as Nell began scrubbing the kitchen sink with gusto. Then, feeling guilty, she stood up and asked how she could help.

"Oh no... you need to rest, dear," said Nell firmly. "Go into the sitting room and lie down on the sofa."

"I'm fine," Poppy insisted. "They wouldn't have discharged me from the hospital otherwise. The doctor told me that fentanyl is metabolised really quickly by the body and there aren't any after-effects. They only kept Amber in for a bit longer because she's pregnant and they wanted to monitor her for a bit."

"Well, thank goodness that awful Christine woman used fentanyl and not the plant poison she used on Valerie Winkle," said Nell.

Poppy shuddered. "Yes, if it had been aconitine, it would have been a very different story!" She sighed and shook her head. "But you know, now that it's all over, the whole thing feels so surreal. I mean, I just can't believe that Christine was the murderer. It's almost like... like I keep forgetting and have to remind myself again."

"I don't know how," said Nell darkly. "If someone tried to stick *me* in an incinerator, I wouldn't forget that in a hurry. And I was surprised when I heard you talking to that lady inspector earlier. You almost sounded sorry for the woman! Poppy, dear, she tried to kill you."

"Yes, I know, but..." Poppy sighed again. She knew she should have felt angry and vengeful towards Christine, but instead she mainly felt pity. There was something about the other woman's anguish that she could relate to. "I think she's just very messed up inside. You know her father abandoned her and her mother when she was just a little girl? I don't think she's ever got over it. And I wonder if it's a coincidence that her father was a doctor—and John Smitheringale is a doctor too. It's like she projected all her feelings for her father onto him and then, when he dumped her, she completely flipped."

"Ah, I told you, didn't I? I said break-ups are always nasty and bitter. People never just accept things and move on. Oh no... especially if they were the one who was dumped," said Nell, nodding her head sagely.

"But lots of people break up every day," Poppy argued. "They don't all go around trying to murder people in retaliation."

Still, she had to admit to herself that perhaps if she had paid more attention to Nell's romantic musings for once, she might have picked up on Christine's motives sooner.

"Ah well... that will do for now," said Nell, standing back from the sink and surveying it critically. "I'll have to wait until next week when I move in to give it a proper clean."

A proper clean? Poppy stared incredulously at the sparkling sink. *What's she going to do? Scour it with a nuclear missile?*

"When I've packed up the London house and come back with all my things, I'll have more cleaning equipment and I'll be able to tackle this place properly," said Nell, looking around the kitchen with anticipation.

Then she beamed at Poppy. "Oh, but I can't believe that you've already lined up a job for me, dear! That is just so wonderful! I can't tell you how much it's been worrying me... and now to think that I'll be able to move here and just go straight into a new job." She shook her head in admiration. "And I only told you about my redundancy earlier this week—how on earth did you manage to find me a new position so quickly?"

By selling my soul to the devil... or to Hubert Leach, which is close enough, thought Poppy wryly. She dreaded the day when her cousin would call in his favour and she wondered with trepidation what it would be. Still, seeing Nell's happy, smiling face made her feel that it was all worth it.

CHAPTER TWENTY-EIGHT

The next morning, Poppy made her way across the village to the Smitheringales' house and was surprised when Amber opened the door.

"Oh, you're up! I thought you'd be resting," she said.

Amber rolled her eyes. "Don't you start as well!" she said with good-natured protest. "I've had John fussing over me all night. You'd think I was dying or something!"

"Well, you did have quite a nasty experience," said Poppy, surprised at how quickly the other girl seemed to have bounced back.

"Yes, but I feel fine now," Amber insisted. "And the doctors said that the baby is fine too."

"Oh, that's great! That was the reason I popped over, actually—just to see how you were doing. I knew the hospital was keeping you in for an extra night."

"Yes, I came home this morning. John wanted me to return to London, but I told him I wanted to come back here..."

They were interrupted by an anxious male voice:

"Amber? What are you doing up? Sweetheart, I told you not to answer the door—" John Smitheringale broke off as he came into the foyer and saw Poppy.

He looked so different from the last time she'd seen him that she was a bit shocked. His face was pale and haggard, with dark circles under his eyes and lines of strain around his mouth, and his usual air of smug confidence was gone. Instead, he looked unsure and almost cowed, like someone who'd had the stuffing beaten out of him. You would almost have thought that *he* was the one who'd just had a brush with death, and not Amber.

"Oh... hello, Poppy," he said, looking very uncomfortable.

Poppy realised that he must have been feeling guilty and ashamed at her knowing about his affair with Christine, and how his actions had inadvertently put her and his own wife in danger. For the first time since she'd met him, she felt a flicker of genuine empathy for John Smitheringale.

To fill the awkward silence, Poppy held up the bunch of flowers she had brought. "Here... these are for you," she said to Amber. "I'm afraid it's not a very professional arrangement; I just cut various things I found in the cottage garden and—"

"Oh, I *love* them!" cried Amber, taking the bunch and burying her nose in the scented blooms. "There's just something so wonderful about fresh-cut garden flowers—they're so much nicer than those stiff, artificial bouquets you get from florists. Oh, and I've got the perfect vase for them too... Come in! Come in! I was just about to have a cup of coffee, actually, so it's perfect timing. Would you like a cup? Or perhaps you'd prefer tea?"

"Er... tea would be great, but honestly, you don't have to bother—I wasn't intending to stay. I just wanted to see how you were—"

"Don't be silly! It's lovely to have some normal company. All I've had so far is John fussing around me like an old hen," she said, sending her husband a mischievous look.

Her husband cleared his throat. "Yes, well... I've got some things to finish up in my study so... um... I'll leave you girls to it."

Poppy watched thoughtfully as he hurried from the room. She had been surprised by Amber's manner. Somehow, she didn't think the old John Smitheringale would have put up with his wife's teasing like that. It was almost as if there was a subtle but meaningful shift in the dynamics of the relationship.

Bustling happily ahead, Amber led the way to the huge living room at the back of the house. The

French doors were thrown open as usual, giving a view of the whole back garden, and Poppy noted uneasily that the flower bed—with its strange construction of canvas garden bags draped over wooden stakes—was easily visible from the living room.

Amber saw her looking and said with a laugh, "What *are* you doing in the flower bed, Poppy? Oh, don't worry, I've been very good—I haven't even taken a peek—but I'm dying to know what you're hiding under there! Are you wrapping it up like a present, and then planning to surprise me when the whole bed is finished?"

"Er..." Poppy licked dry lips. Then she took a deep breath and said in a rush: "Actually... Amber, I need to tell you something. I... I messed up a bit when I was planting the bed—well, actually, I messed up a lot." She gave a nervous laugh. "I thought I knew what I was doing but... but I didn't. The plants are suffering from transplant shock. They've shrivelled up and their leaves are falling off."

Amber's blue eyes were wide with surprise.

"I've asked Joe and he thinks I might be able to save them," Poppy added hurriedly. "I'm keeping them hydrated and out of the sun—that's why I rigged up that shade over the bed. But if they don't recover... if they die..." She forced herself to meet the other girl's eyes. "I'll replace all of them myself. I promise."

Amber was silent for a moment, then to Poppy's shock, she gave a little laugh.

"It's... it's not a joke," said Poppy, looking at the other girl hesitantly.

"Oh, no... no, I'm sure you're serious. You look so upset." Amber shook her head and smiled.

Poppy blinked. "You're... you're not angry?"

Amber laughed again. "Poppy! You do realise that we both nearly died? I mean, twenty-four hours ago, we were on our way to an incinerator!"

"Oh... yeah..." said Poppy with a sheepish laugh. "It's just... I felt terrible that I was lying to you—"

"Yes, well, if I'm being honest, I probably would have been a bit annoyed about that..." Amber chuckled. "But you know—nearly getting killed really puts things in perspective." She looked at Poppy curiously. "Am I that scary? Why did you feel that you had to lie?"

"I was just... I didn't mean to lie! I meant to tell you everything when you were asking me about the screen the first time... but then somehow, I don't know—these words just came out of my mouth and then it was too late..." Poppy heaved a sigh and added with a shamefaced grin, "I guess I was too embarrassed to admit that I'd mucked up so badly, after pretending I knew what to do. I should have told you from the start that I'm a complete beginner. It's just that this was my first gardening job and I really wanted to impress you..." She gave the other girl a grateful smile. "Anyway, thanks...

for being so understanding."

Amber put a hand on her belly. "Well… I'm a complete beginner when it comes to motherhood and I'm sure I'm going to muck up too. I'm hoping that people will show me a bit of understanding as well." Then she gave Poppy an impish grin and added, "Besides, how can I be angry with you? You're the person who saved my life."

"Oh… it wasn't… I mean, I didn't really do anything," stammered Poppy.

Amber opened her eyes wide. "What do you mean? If you hadn't worked out that the murderer was Christine and rushed to find me, I would probably be a pile of ashes in an incinerator somewhere."

"Ugh." Poppy shuddered and wondered again how the other girl could be so blasé about their whole ordeal. There was obviously a steely core beneath that pretty, blonde exterior.

Amber put a hand on her arm. "Listen… you know, John had already decided on the names for the baby—he said that if it was a girl, we would call her Henrietta—but I've told him that if the baby is a girl, I want to call her Poppy." She smiled. "If you don't mind?"

"Oh! No, of course, I don't mind! I'm… I'm really touched," said Poppy, taken completely by surprise. She had been expecting to be chastised and fired—not to be honoured with a namesake! "But… is John okay about that? I mean, I thought you said he normally likes to get his own way—"

"Oh, John's changed a lot in the last couple of days. I think this whole thing with Christine has knocked him for six. He told me this morning that when the police rang him and told him what had happened to me, he was absolutely terrified. He raced straight up from London—he probably broke the speed limit the whole way!" Amber gave a whimsical smile. "I think he didn't realise how important his family—me and the baby—was to him, until he almost lost us."

Perhaps he'll even change his womanising ways? wondered Poppy. Then she laughed cynically to herself. What was she thinking? A leopard never changed its spots. Still, as she was getting up to leave, she was surprised to see John come out of his study and politely accompany his wife to see her to the door.

"Oh, I'll let John see you out, if you don't mind. I need to pop to the loo—for the tenth time this morning," said Amber with a rueful laugh. "Why didn't anyone tell me that being pregnant made your bladder shrink to the size of a pea?" She gave Poppy a little wave. "I'll see you tomorrow."

"You... you still want me to do the rest of the garden?" said Poppy.

"Of course! You're not getting out of it that easily," said Amber with a wink.

Then she disappeared up the stairs, leaving Poppy and John alone in the foyer. The cardiologist looked terribly uncomfortable and shamefaced, so much so that Poppy felt sorry for him and quickly turned to go. But he put out a hand to stop her.

"Wait, Poppy..." There was an awkward pause, then he cleared his throat and said: "I wanted to tell you that... I'm... I'm sorry you got involved and... er... I wanted to thank you also for—"

"Oh no, no—there's nothing to thank me for," she cut in quickly.

"No, there is. I owe you a huge debt of gratitude for saving my wife's life. If there's anything I can ever do to repay you..."

The words were a bit pompous but his voice was sincere, and when Poppy looked at him, she couldn't see any trace of his usual smug arrogance. She recalled what Nick had said about his friend and had to admit that perhaps he was right: John Smitheringale wasn't an evil man—just a flawed one. In fact, she felt slightly ashamed now for having suspected him of murder.

The thought made her remember something else and she said: "Actually, there *is* something—a question I'd like to ask you. A few days ago, I saw you in Oxford. You were going into a TCM clinic... I just wondered what you were doing there? The reason I'm asking—" she added hurriedly, "—is because I thought you might have been going there to get hold of some aconitine."

John's mouth dropped open. "You thought I was the murderer?"

Poppy gave a sheepish smile. “Yes. I overheard you and Valerie arguing on the first day I came here, and she made that comment about your ‘addiction’. It was obvious she had some kind of hold over you. I thought maybe she was blackmailing you.”

John had flushed at her mention of “addiction”, and he said hurriedly, like someone keen to change the subject, “There was nothing sinister about my visit. I was simply going to see one of the TCM practitioners.”

“But...” Poppy frowned. “You looked really furtive, like you didn’t want anyone to see you.”

John cleared his throat again and said gruffly, “I’ve always been very vocal about my contempt for traditional Chinese remedies—I was even interviewed about it for various journals and TV talk shows. But I... er... have been suffering from some eczema on my hands which just wouldn’t clear up. It was really frustrating and I had already tried every drug and treatment available to Western medicine. Then I heard about how successful TCM is in treating skin conditions. So I...”

“You thought you’d try it—but you didn’t want anyone to see you eating your words.”

He gave an embarrassed shrug. “Yes, pretty much. I suppose you’re thinking I’m a stupid sod for being too proud to admit that I was wrong.”

Poppy laughed suddenly. *If only he knew...* “No, actually—I can empathise. Really.”

She smiled at him—the first genuine smile she had given him—and thought that perhaps John Smitheringale wasn't so bad after all...

CHAPTER TWENTY-NINE

When Poppy got back to Hollyhock Cottage, she was surprised to find the air filled with the delicious smell of fresh baking and she walked into the sitting room to find the cushions plumped up, the curtains drawn back to let the sunshine in, and the coffee table covered with a clean cloth and laid with an assortment of mismatched china. In the kitchen, she found freshly baked scones, flapjacks, and shortbread biscuits laid out on the counter.

"What's going on? Why have you baked so many things?" she asked Nell, who was busily poking holes in a lemon drizzle cake.

Her old friend looked up and beamed. "We're having a tea party!"

"We're *what?*"

"Yes, well, I thought it was a nice way to meet

your neighbours on either side, dear, so I popped over first thing this morning and left notes in both their letterboxes, inviting them to come over."

"Oh... that was nice of you, but I don't know if anyone will come," said Poppy gently. "I mean, Bertie might—if he's not immersed in some mad experiment or other—but I doubt that Nick will."

"And why not?" Nell placed her hands on her hips.

"I just... He's a writer. They're not really the sociable kind."

"Oh, surely not all writers are the same—"

"Besides, I'm not sure if Nick is always very good company," said Poppy, making a face. "He's terribly moody, and blows hot and cold from one minute to the next."

Nell gave her a speculative look. "I didn't realise that you knew him so well."

"No... well, I... I don't really *know* him. We've bumped into each other a few times, that's all." Poppy added hurriedly, in case Nell wondered why they were running into each other so often. "My grandmother was quite friendly with Nick and invited him to come over to the cottage gardens any time he liked. Apparently, something about this place really helps him think, especially when he's stuck on a plot. So that's why I've seen him sometimes—"

"You mean he comes over here when you're alone? At night?" said Nell, looking scandalised.

"Not in the house—just in the gardens! But yes, he's been over at night, when I was here alone..." Poppy gave an exasperated laugh. "For goodness' sake, Nell—this isn't the eighteenth century! I don't need a chaperone."

"Hmm..." Nell pursed her lips. "Well, it's a good thing I'm going to meet him today and get a good look at him," she said, like someone contemplating picking out a criminal from an identity parade.

"He probably won't come," muttered Poppy, thinking that it was probably a good thing.

Nell pushed a strand of grey hair out of her face with the back of her hand, leaving a smear of flour on her forehead. "I must say, Poppy, this old oven might not look like much but it does a fantastic job. Look how evenly baked and golden everything is. I've only done some quick recipes this morning, but I'm looking forward to trying some of my fancier cakes and buns after I move in."

"Mm..." said Poppy, only half listening as she approached the counter and reached for one of the scones. The rich, buttery smell was mouth-watering, and after the measly meals she had prepared for herself in the last few weeks, the thought of sampling some home baking was heavenly.

"*Ah-ah...* wait until the visitors come," said Nell, giving her hand a mock slap.

"Oh Nell... I'm starving and I told you, I doubt anyone will come—" Poppy stopped in surprise as she heard the front doorbell ring.

Nell gave a complacent smile as she reached over, picked up a flapjack, and handed it to Poppy. "You were saying, dear?"

Poppy grinned, took the flapjack from Nell, and went to answer the door. As she munched on the sweet, chewy bar, warm from the oven and redolent with rolled oats, butter, brown sugar, and golden syrup, she was reminded again why Nell's flapjacks were legendary. She was still chewing with her mouth full when she opened the door and found Nick Forrest on the doorstep, looking cool and suave in dark jeans and a crisp cotton shirt, with the sleeves rolled up at the elbows.

"Oh! You came," she said stupidly.

He raised an eyebrow, his eyes twinkling, "Wasn't I supposed to?"

"No... er... I just didn't think... um... come in," stammered Poppy.

"*N-ow?*" said a big ginger tomcat, strolling past his owner's legs and walking into the house as if they had all been waiting for his arrival.

Nick grinned. He seemed to be in an unusually good mood. "Well, Oren did tell me that the invitation was really for him, but he said I could come as his guest."

Poppy led the way into the sitting room where they found that the ginger tom had already made himself comfortable in his favourite armchair. This left them only the sofa and Poppy perched nervously next to Nick as he sat down.

"Um... would you like some tea?" she asked, her voice stilted. Their previous meetings had always been a bit ad hoc—this was the first time they were meeting in any kind of "formal" social setting—and suddenly she felt stiff and awkward.

Before he could reply, Nell bustled into the room, carrying plates of scones and biscuits, and an old teapot with a chipped spout.

"So... you're the crime writer, eh?" she said, fixing Nick with a hard stare.

Nick looked nonplussed. "Uh... yes, I am." Then he recovered his usual aplomb, held out his hand, and gave her his most charming smile. "My name's Nick. And you must be Poppy's friend from London... Mrs Hopkins, I believe?"

"Hmm." Nell softened slightly but her eyes remained suspicious as she took his hand. "You can call me Nell."

"I understand that you'll be coming to stay with Poppy here at Hollyhock Cottage?"

"That's right." She shot him a pointed look. "So any man who thinks he can take advantage of Poppy just because she's living here alone can think again—"

"Ah—thanks, Nell!" Poppy interrupted, reaching to grab the teapot. "Um... do you want to get the rest of the things while I help Nick to some tea?"

"I've got some tarts in the oven, and the icing to put on the lemon drizzle cake, so I'll be a few minutes," said Nell. "But I'll be back soon." She gave Nick another withering stare, then turned and retreated into the kitchen.

Poppy poured the tea and glanced at the man beside her, who was still staring at the door through which Nell had disappeared. "Er... sorry, I'm sure she didn't mean—"

"Hmm? What?" Nick blinked, coming out of his daze. "She's *fantastic*! Absolutely perfect!"

Poppy looked at him in bewilderment. "I'm sorry?"

"For a novel! She'd make a great character in a story," said Nick enthusiastically. "That attitude—and that face, with those hard, suspicious eyes and pursed mouth..." His own eyes took on a faraway expression. "Hmm... yes, I could have her as a key witness in the murder... maybe as a cook... or an old bag lady..."

Poppy glanced quickly at the doorway that led to the back of the house and hoped that Nell couldn't hear. Finding out that Nick was casting her as an old bag lady in one of his novels would be the last straw!

"Oh, I've just remembered—I know the usual thing is to bring chocolates or flowers, but I thought you might enjoy this more." Nick pulled something out of his jacket pocket and handed it to her.

It was a slim, hard package, wrapped in brown paper and tied up with string, like an old-fashioned book parcel. In fact, it *was* a book. Poppy peeled back the wrapping and gazed with delight at the cover of the hardback decorated with plant illustrations and the title: *Poisonous Plants of the British Isles.*

"I hope it doesn't come across as bad taste, given recent events," said Nick, his mouth twisting in a smile. "But I thought you might like that for your plant library."

"Oooh, yes—thank you!" cried Poppy, opening the book and flipping through the pages eagerly. "I can't wait to sit down and read this from cover to cover… Oh look—here's *Aconitum*!" She paused on a page and began to read out loud: "*Often called the Queen of Poisons,* Aconitum napellus *is one of the most toxic plants known to man—even brushing against the buds can be deadly. Legend has it that it grew from the spittle of Cerberus, the three-headed hound of hell, after the fearsome beast was lured from the Underworld by the hero Hercules.*" She looked up at Nick, glowing. "I can't wait to take this to bed!"

He picked up his teacup and raised a mocking eyebrow. "And here I was, all these years, thinking that it was chocolates and roses that did it for women…"

Poppy glanced at him quickly. Was Nick flirting with her? Surely not!

"I can't wait to show this to Bertie when he arrives," she said, pretending to ignore the comment. "He was telling me all about *Aconitum* the other day and I'm sure he'll have something to say about—"

"Bertie?" Nick had paused in the act of reaching for a scone and now turned a frowning face to her. "Bertram Noble is coming here? Now?"

"Yes, Nell thought it would be nice to meet my neighbours, so she invited both—Wait! What are you doing?" she cried as Nick put his cup down with a rattle of china and stood up.

"I'm leaving. I'm not going to sit here and have tea with that man."

"What?" Poppy stared at him in disbelief. "But... why?"

Nick gave her a curt nod. "Please make my excuses to Nell." He turned and headed for the door.

Poppy sprang up. "This is crazy... you're not seriously leaving? I don't understand—why do you hate Bertie so much?" she cried angrily. "What's he ever done to you?"

Nick stopped and swung around. His dark eyes were filled with some unfathomable emotion.

"He's my father."

Then he turned and strode out of the room. A minute later, the front door slammed, leaving Poppy staring open-mouthed after him.

CHAPTER THIRTY

It took Poppy several minutes before she realised that she was still standing in the middle of the room, staring at the empty doorway. She hesitated for a moment, then dashed outside. She had thought that she might still catch Nick on the path to the front gate but there was no sign of him. He must have moved really fast! She wondered whether to chase him back to his house (assuming that he had gone back there). As she was debating what to do, she heard the sound of an engine in the lane and, moments later, a car door slamming.

A slim, elegant woman with dark hair and a quiet beauty appeared on the other side of the garden gate. Poppy's face broke into a smile as she recognised Suzanne Whittaker, and she hurried down the path to meet the detective inspector.

"Suzanne! How nice to see you! Come in; we're actually having a sort of 'tea party' so it's perfect timing—"

"Oh, I'm afraid I can't stay long. I just happened to be in the village to speak to Desmond Fothergill and thought I'd pop in to see how you were."

"Oh... thanks... that's really sweet of you," said Poppy, touched. "I'm fine. No after-effects at all." She looked at the other woman curiously. "Er... you said you were speaking to Fothergill?"

Suzanne gave her a measured look. "Yes, we found some drafts of letters in Valerie's house that indicate she was blackmailing several people... but somehow I have a feeling you already knew about them?"

Poppy could feel her cheeks heating up and she tried hard not to look guilty.

"And yes, you were right," Suzanne continued. "Fothergill was one of her victims. There were no names on the letters, but we checked Valerie's bank account and found regular payments from several people—including Fothergill—going back several months."

"But he wasn't the murderer in the end," said Poppy, feeling suddenly sorry for the businessman. "Do you have to expose him?"

"No. He wasn't involved in Valerie's murder and I am happy to respect his privacy. I just like to tie up loose ends for myself, which is why I went to see him. But I've promised to keep his name and any details of the blackmail out of the press and public record."

"So that *was* him on Valerie's doorstep the night she was poisoned?"

"Yes, apparently he'd thought—naïvely perhaps—that if he was nice to her, he might be able to appeal to her better nature and convince her to stop the extortion." Suzanne gave a cynical laugh. "Sadly, I don't think Valerie would have been very inclined to be compassionate. She was making a nice little packet from all these payouts... I was quite surprised, actually, at how many people in the village were involved."

Poppy couldn't help remembering Nick's comment about the most respectable, genteel-looking places and people having the most secrets.

"Um... I don't suppose Joe Fabbri was one of those people?" she asked suddenly.

Suzanne looked at her in surprise. "Yes, he was, actually. I've spoken to him too. Apparently, when she was spying around the village, Valerie once saw him knock over an expensive antique vase in one of the houses he was working at. It smashed and Fabbri was terrified of being asked to replace such an expensive item, so he lied and told the owners that a freak breeze had come in the window and blown it over. And he'd been paying a large portion of his earnings to Valerie each month, for her to keep quiet about that." She narrowed her eyes. "How did you know about him?"

"Oh... um... I just wondered, because I thought it was strange that he was cleaning Valerie's tools for her—given that he didn't like her much." Poppy said lamely. "I mean—I thought it might be the same thing as Desmond Fothergill trying to be nice to her..."

Obviously, Suzanne didn't know about Joe breaking into Valerie's house that night and Poppy knew that she couldn't mention it without admitting her own trespass. In any case, she didn't want to land Joe in even more trouble. She might never know what he had really been doing that night, but she could guess that he had probably been searching for any blackmail letters that Valerie might have kept, in case his name was mentioned and he was linked to the woman's murder.

The memory of the letters made her think of something else and she asked: "Suzanne, I was wondering—what's going to happen to the things in Valerie's house now?"

"Well, I imagine the executor of her estate will sort things out. She was a spinster, with no close family, and I think most of the estate will go to various gardening charities. I believe your cousin, Hubert Leach, has already contacted the executor about handling the sale of her property."

Ah, good old Hubert, thought Poppy, rolling her eyes internally. She said: "Well... um... I believe Valerie had some seed packets and I was thinking—if her executor wouldn't mind—I'd love to have some, to plant in the cottage garden here. It would be a nice way to remember her—a sort of legacy. I mean, she was a really annoying woman, but she did give me good gardening advice, even though I didn't realise it at the time."

"As it happens, those seed packets are in police custody because they were where the blackmail letters were found... which I suspect you already knew," said Suzanne, giving Poppy another wry look. "The executor is not interested in having them back—so you're welcome to the whole lot." She leaned back and shook her head, a resigned smile on her lips. "You know, Poppy, one of these days, I'd love to find out how you and Nick knew so much about Valerie's blackmailing operation."

Poppy flushed. "Oh... speaking of Nick—can I ask you something about him?"

Suzanne nodded, her expression curious.

"It's about him and Bertie—Dr Bertram Noble." Poppy looked at Suzanne hesitantly. "Did you know that Bertie is Nick's *father*?"

Suzanne sighed. "Yes. I did."

"Why is Nick so hostile towards Bertie? Why does he hate his own father so much?"

Suzanne hesitated. "You'd better ask Nick directly. It's a personal thing and I'm not sure it's my place to tell you." She gave Poppy a sad smile. "Although don't be surprised if Nick refuses to talk about it. And now, I'd better go."

They walked towards the garden gate together.

"Thanks for coming to see me. Maybe..." Poppy looked shyly at the other woman. "Maybe we could go out for a coffee together sometime?"

"Yes, I'd like that," said Suzanne, returning her smile. "You've got my number. I might be on a case and working all hours known to man—and woman!—but give me a ring or send me a text, and we'll see if we can arrange a time. I know a great little tearoom just outside Oxford where they do fantastic scones."

***

Poppy stood at the gate and watched until Suzanne had pulled out of the lane before walking back to the cottage. She was just entering the front door when she heard a screech come from the rear of the house. She broke into a run and burst into the kitchen to find Nell waving a broom and yelling at an old man with a mop of wild grey hair, who was trying to come in the door from the greenhouse. He was carrying a rat in one hand, an umbrella in the other, and had a pair of swimming goggles on his head—and a little terrier at his heels.

"...did you think you could come sneaking in here without me seeing? Get out! Get out, you filthy tramp!" Nell shouted. "I saw you from the window—yes, I saw you climbing through that hole in the wall! Thought you could creep onto the property from the back, did you? You wait until I call the police—"

"But I don't understand... where's Poppy?" asked Bertie, looking bewildered. "She invited me and Einstein for a tea party—"

"*Ruff... Ruff-ruff... RUFF!*" Einstein barked excitedly as he ran in circles around them.

"Nell—stop, stop!" cried Poppy, wading into the melee. She grabbed the broom, trying to pull it out of Nell's hands, and shouted to make herself heard. "That's not a tramp—that's Bertie!"

Nell stopped in confusion. "Wh-what?"

Poppy cleared her throat and said, gesturing towards the old man in front of them: "Nell... meet our neighbour, Dr Bertram Noble. There's a gap in the wall between our properties—that's the hole you saw him coming through. We use it as an easy way to come and go." She turned to the old inventor. "Bertie—this is my friend Nell Hopkins, who will be coming to live with me."

Bertie peered at Nell. "You're very loud, aren't you? Almost like a harpy."

Nell bristled. "What did you call me?" Then her gaze dropped to his hands and she took a hasty step back, letting out a loud screech. "Is that a... a *live rat*?"

Bertie beamed and held up the albino rat. "Oh yes, this is Celsius, one of my test rats. He's been missing his friend, Fahrenheit, you see—unfortunately, we lost Fahrenheit in Mr Fothergill's house—and I didn't want Celsius to be lonely, so

I've been taking him everywhere with me."

"I'm not having a rat in this house!" cried Nell, looking at the furry creature in revulsion.

"Oh, don't worry—he's very well trained and never bites. Well, at least, not very hard," Bertie assured her. "In fact, I've even trained him to retrieve—"

"*N-o-oowwww!*"

Poppy turned around to see that Oren had followed her into the kitchen. He was standing next to her now, his yellow eyes dilated almost black and his tail lashing from side to side as he stared at the rat.

Poppy turned hastily back to Bertie. "Er... Bertie, I think you'd better—"

Too late. With a yowl of delight, Oren charged across the room. The rat squeaked in alarm and struggled madly, wriggling out of Bertie's hands. It dropped to the floor and ran straight for the nearest cover—which happened to be Nell's skirt.

Nell shrieked and hopped from foot to foot, swinging her broom wildly. Oren gave another excited yowl and chased after the rat, his whiskers bristling—and Einstein sprang after the cat, barking at the top of his voice.

Poppy felt an overwhelming urge to burst out laughing. The whole scene was so surreal, with the rat-cat-dog train going around and around the room... and Nell waving her broom... and Bertie ducking and trying to catch the rat. It was absolute pandemonium.

At last, Bertie managed to corner the rat, whilst Oren and Einstein were busy yelling insults at each other.

"Oh no—don't use anything from the kitchen! I've just scrubbed and washed everything and I'm not getting rat germs on it!" cried Nell, watching in horror as Bertie attempted to trap the rat with a colander. She beckoned urgently to Poppy. "Quick, dear—go into the greenhouse and see if you can find anything to trap the rat with."

Poppy hurried into the greenhouse extension at the back of the cottage. After a moment of hunting around, she found an old wire basket that could double up as a temporary cage. She grabbed it and was just about to return to the kitchen when something on the workbench caught her eye.

Shoots. Tiny green shoots pushing their way up through the soil, in the trays lining the bench.

"Oh!" Poppy stopped and stared at them.

It was the second batch of seeds she had planted. After sowing them and watering them, she had completely forgotten about them in the chaos of the last few days. Now, she approached the bench and stared at the seedlings in wonder. They were absolutely beautiful: soft, translucent green, with tiny leaves just unfurling from the dainty stems. They looked strong and healthy—and full of promise.

As she stared at them, Poppy felt a smile spread

across her face. There were still so many hurdles ahead of her: she had no idea how she was going to resurrect the garden nursery business, how she was going to grow anything to sell this late in the season, with winter just around the corner... or how she was going to support herself in the meantime.

But instead of panic and despair, she felt a glimmer of hope. She didn't have all the answers yet, but looking down at the sturdy little seedlings, she felt suddenly confident that the answers would be there—when she went searching for them.

THE END

ABOUT THE AUTHOR

USA Today bestselling author H.Y. Hanna writes funny and intriguing British cozy mysteries, set in Oxford and the beautiful English Cotswolds. Her books include the Oxford Tearoom Mysteries, the 'Bewitched by Chocolate' Mysteries and the English Cottage Garden Mysteries—as well as romantic suspense and children's mystery novels. After graduating from Oxford University, Hsin-Yi tried her hand at a variety of jobs, before returning to her first love: writing. She worked as a freelance writer for several years and has won awards for her novels, poetry, short stories and journalism.

A globe-trotter all her life, Hsin-Yi has lived in a variety of cultures, from Dubai to Auckland, London to New Jersey, but is now happily settled in Perth, Western Australia, with her husband and a rescue kitty named Muesli. You can learn more about her (and the real-life Muesli who inspired the cat character in the story) and her other books at: **www.hyhanna.com**.

Sign up to her newsletter to be notified of new releases, exclusive giveaways and other book news! Go to: **www.hyhanna.com/newsletter**

ACKNOWLEDGMENTS

Thank you to my lovely beta readers: Basma Alwesh, Connie Leap and Charles Winthrop, for always finding time to fit me into their busy schedules and for investing so much time and energy into my books. Their thoughtful feedback is always so helpful in making each book the best it can be. I am always grateful to my editor and proofreader, too, for being such a great team to work with.

And last but not least—I can never thank my wonderful husband enough for always being there for me to lean on. I could never do this without his unwavering support, encouragement and enthusiasm. He is one man in a million.

35326593R00188

Made in the USA
San Bernardino, CA
09 May 2019